Rockin' Road Trip

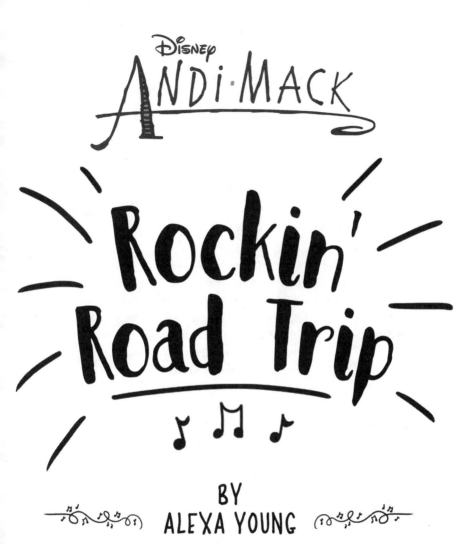

Disney
ANDI·MACK

Rockin' Road Trip

BY
ALEXA YOUNG

Based on the series created by Terri Minsky

DISNEP PRESS
Los Angeles • New York

Printed in the United States of America
First Hardcover Edition, October 2018
1 3 5 7 9 10 8 6 4 2
Library of Congress Control Number: 2018936686
ISBN 978-1-368-02431-0
FAC-020093-18243

For more Disney Press fun, visit www.disneybooks.com
Visit DisneyChannel.com

THIS LABEL APPLIES TO TEXT STOCK

FOR MY PARENTS, WHO TOOK ME ON COUNTLESS
ADVENTURES . . . AND FOR JOEL AND JACK, WHO
MAKE EVERY DAY AN ADVENTURE

—A.Y.

Chapter 1

Walking home from school with her two best friends at her sides, Andi Mack couldn't stop smiling. She wasn't sure why, but she had the overwhelming sense that something incredible was about to happen—something even more incredible than all the things that had already happened.

"Okay, *what* is going on with you?" Buffy Driscoll asked, shooting an amused look at Andi, who was practically skipping at that point.

"Honestly?" Andi flashed an even bigger grin but didn't want to jinx the looming excitement—whatever it might be. "I have no clue!"

"Ah." Cyrus Goodman nodded, channeling the wisdom of his parents and stepparents, all four of whom were psychotherapists. "Forgive my chutzpah, but I believe *I* know."

"You do?" Buffy and Andi said at the same time, hooking their thumbs through the straps on their backpacks and stopping to stare at Cyrus in mock wonder.

"Also, what is 'chutzpah'?" Andi added.

"It's Yiddish for 'guts,'" Cyrus said.

"Ew!" Andi cringed.

"No—not like *intestines*," Cyrus explained. "It means boldness, courage, *grit*."

"Yeah!" Buffy tossed her head back and put a hand on her hip. "It's one of my favorite Yiddish words, obvs."

"Speaking of Yiddish," Andi said, glancing at Cyrus, "I can't believe your Bar Mitzvah is coming up so soon!"

"And I still don't have a *thing* to wear," Buffy added.

"Me neither," Andi replied, frowning at Buffy. "Should we make a shopping date?"

Buffy bit her lip. "I'm not sure. I have to check my practice schedule for basketball, ya know?"

"It's okay," Andi said. "We can figure it out later—or maybe I can just get Bowie to go shopping with me. He's surprisingly good with fashion direction."

"You sure?" Buffy scowled.

"Totally!" Andi insisted, turning to Cyrus and quickly changing the subject, still eager to hear his take on her current mood—which was, admittedly, pretty great. Hence the smiling. "So, what *do* you think is going on with me?"

"Well . . ." Cyrus looked up at the sunny, cloudless sky as a cool breeze rustled through the leaves of the lush green trees. He stretched his arms high and spun around before presenting the big reveal with a thick British accent: "You're experiencing *gratitude*, luv—a complete and utter appreciation for, well, let's see . . . Good weather! Good health! Good clothes! Good hair—*obviously*! And most of all . . . ?"

"Yes?" Andi and Buffy widened their eyes impatiently as they waited for their goofball friend to share his final observation.

"Good*man*," Cyrus finally said, extending an arm and offering his most smoldering James Bond–style gaze as he shook Andi's hand and then Buffy's. "*Cyrus* Goodman."

Buffy rolled her eyes and laughed. "Oh, my good man," she replied, adopting a British accent of her own. "That *must* be it!"

"Definitely!" Andi grinned and waved goodbye to her friends before turning toward the redbrick building with yellow trim and racing up the three concrete steps leading to apartment 108B.

"Good day!" Andi practically sang after she opened the French doors leading into the living room, where she found Bex sitting on the olive-hued velvet sleeper sofa, reading a magazine.

"Uh . . . *'good day'*?" Bex looked up from her magazine with a smirk. "Shall I make us some tea and crumpets?"

Andi giggled. "No. Sorry. Cyrus was just being . . . Cyrus, and then we all kind of got into it."

"Ah," Bex said with a nod, turning her attention back to the magazine.

Andi wrinkled her nose, sensing a weird energy. It was like the moment she had walked in, her mysteriously good mood got swept away and locked outside.

Maybe it's a blood sugar thing, Andi thought. She headed for the kitchen and grabbed a box of animal crackers from the shelf next to the pale yellow retro stove, then returned to the living room and flopped down on the chair by the sofa.

"Hungry?" Andi asked, holding out the box for Bex.

Bex shook her head without even looking up from her magazine.

"Gee . . . that must be a *really* fascinating article," Andi said with a shrug, slightly irritated. She popped a few cookies into her mouth and focused on savoring every crumb, determined to maintain the attitude of gratitude Cyrus had observed. But it was no use; she couldn't recapture the adrenaline that had been pumping through her veins mere moments before.

"So, what do you want to do this weekend?" Andi finally asked. Maybe Bex had something fabulous planned and Andi's subconscious had been sensing it earlier.

"A whole lot of *nothing*!" Bex replied with a huge smile.

"Really?" Andi puffed out her lower lip and crossed her arms. "But it's Friday! You don't want to get out of here? Do something fun?"

"Maybe." Bex tilted her head, considering Andi's

words, and then added, "But staying home doing nothing can be fun!"

"Seriously?" Andi exhaled loudly. "Won't you be bored?"

"Nah. It's been a busy week. Time for some R and R!" Bex stretched out on the couch and draped the open magazine over her eyes like a sleep mask.

Andi scowled. "Aren't you *already* bored?"

The room was silent for what felt like hours, and Andi wondered if Bex really had fallen asleep—but then Bex jumped to her feet, letting the magazine fall to the hardwood floor. "Wait . . ." Bex said, visibly unsettled. "Are *you* bored?"

Andi scrunched up her face and thought about how strange it would be to admit such a thing. The fact was life had been anything *but* boring in the months since Bex had returned to Shadyside, rolling up in front of the Mack house on her motorcycle and announcing that she would be staying. She had arrived the day before Andi's thirteenth birthday, and Andi could not have been more thrilled about the news.

After all, it was Bex: the person Andi had always known as her ultracool older sister, who had left home to go on all sorts of crazy adventures when Andi was a baby—and Andi had already decided that when she turned thirteen, she was going to take a page out of the same thrill-seeking book. She had even saved up her cat-sitting money and bought an electric scooter *without asking permission*—and then, *poof!* Her big sister cruised up like some sort of black-leather-clad fairy godmother, just in time to help make Andi's rebel-with-a-cause dreams come true!

Then, the next night, on Andi's thirteenth birthday, Bex revealed something seriously crazy: she told Andi that she wasn't her sister at all—she was her *mother*. Andi was stunned, to say the least. That meant Celia "CeCe" Mack, the woman Andi had thought was her mother, was really her *grandmother* . . . and Henry "Ham" Mack, the man she had thought was her father, was actually her *grandfather*.

Things got even crazier from there. Andi met and started spending time with her real father, Bowie Quinn, a free-spirited musician who was clearly Bex's soul mate, even though Bex turned him down when he asked her to marry him. Andi also got her first real boyfriend: Jonah Beck—as in *the* Jonah Beck, who was basically the cutest, most charming, most popular eighth grader at Jefferson Middle School. Even though Jonah and Andi were only friends these days, that might never have happened if Bex hadn't arranged a Frisbee lesson with Jonah for Andi's birthday present. (Jonah was the founder and captain of the Space Otters, the school's Ultimate Frisbee team, which Andi even joined for a short time.) The craziest part of all? Bex got a job and her own apartment, and Andi moved out of the only home she'd ever known, away from the only parents she'd ever known, and in with Bex—who Andi eventually began calling Mom. *Mom!*

Yet after all the ups, downs, twists, and turns Andi's life had taken with Bex, at that moment in time, with the dust a bit more settled, it all seemed to be screeching to a serious—and, yeah, possibly *snooze-worthy*—stop.

"Seriously, Andi—are you bored?" Bex asked again. She'd never thought she'd be the kind of mom who would have a bored kid.

"Um." Andi fidgeted with a thread on her yellow head-band. "Maybe we're just in a bit of a rut?"

"No." Bex began pacing around the room and shook her head as she continued to mutter, "No, no, no, no, no, no, *no*. You can't be bored! We are fun!"

Then Bex quickly went into full-on fix-it mode, her eyes lighting up each time she tossed out an idea. "We could have a John Hughes movie marathon, with giant buckets of popcorn and all the animal crackers you can eat!"

"Again?" Andi frowned.

"Okay," Bex said, undeterred, "how about if we *go* to the movies and then out for pizza—or to the Spoon if that sounds better?"

Andi's mouth stretched open into a big, long yawn. She tried to cover it up with her hands, but it was too late.

"No!" Bex shrieked, grabbing Andi's shoulders and shaking her. "This isn't happening! You will *not* be bored on my watch!"

But with each activity Bex proposed—playing dice games or card games, going shopping or to the new museum exhibit, flying kites at the park or even doing a mother-daughter at-home spa day—Andi sunk deeper into the chair cushions. It was too weird! It was like Bex was turning into one of those generic moms. Where was the *real* Bex—the one who constantly encouraged Andi to step outside her comfort zone: to throw a house party while Ham and CeCe went out of town, to protest the school dress code by wearing a prison uniform? Where had adventurous, full-of-surprises, *rebellious* Bex gone?

"I know!" Andi suddenly blurted out. "What would you be doing *right now* if I weren't here—like if you were off on one of your adventures, without me in the picture?"

Bex stuffed her hands into the pockets of her army jacket and scowled. "I don't ever want to think about a life without you in the picture . . . *that* would be boring. And awful. And sad."

"But if you *could*," Andi said, pressing her. "Come on! Just for fun . . . pretend I'm not here and you have no responsibilities! Where would you go, what would you do?"

But Bex planted her black motorcycle boots firmly on the floor, her hands on the hips of her distressed jeans, and shook her head. "That's not an option—and it will never be an option again."

Clearly the topic wasn't open for discussion—and Andi had to admit she wasn't entirely bummed about that. She didn't want to think about her life without Bex around, either. Even a not-so-wild-and-crazy Bex was better than no Bex at all.

"Fine," Andi said, pasting on her most convincing smile and grabbing her phone to look up showtimes. "Let's go to the movies."

Chapter 2

"See? Wasn't that fun?" Bex asked as she and Andi exited the movie theater later that night.

Andi stifled yet another yawn—not because the movie had been boring, but probably because it was almost eleven o'clock.

"Okay, that's it—I'm taking you to the Spoon," Bex said. "You're clearly in need of more sugar."

"Seriously?" Andi asked, pulling on her soft pale blue cardigan. "But it's so late, and I already had a ton of candy!"

"*Now* who's being boring?" Bex taunted her.

"Not me!" Andi laughed. "I just meant I thought it was past *your* bedtime. Remember? *You* were the one who wanted to do *a whole lot of nothing*, who said it was *time for some R and R*."

"Huh? *Who* said that?" Bex deadpanned, and then skipped ahead. "I'm wide awake and ready for a shake! Makin' rhymes and feeling fine!"

"Ugh." Andi rolled her eyes, smiling as she caught up to Bex.

But as soon as they arrived at the diner, Andi noticed a poster in the window and stopped short, her heart beginning to race.

"Oh my gosh!" Andi grabbed Bex by the arm and pointed at the poster. "The Mountain Jam Music and Arts Festival is next weekend—and the Renaissance Boys are headlining! Did you know about this?"

"Nope, first I'm hearing of it." Bex took a step toward the purple poster and narrowed her eyes as she scanned the long list of band names. There had to be at least thirty acts playing each day, and the Renaissance Boys were listed at the very top in huge swirly silver letters.

"But you've been to Mountain Jam before—you sent me a scarf from there a few years ago, right?"

"Totally," Bex murmured, getting a dreamy, faraway look in her dark eyes. "I've been lots of times."

"We should go!" Andi started bouncing up and down in her white sneakers. "I mean, we *have* to go—right? I have next Monday off school, so it would be a perfect way to spend the three-day weekend!"

Bex's expression quickly changed from blissful to wistful. "I don't know, Andi. . . ."

"Huh?" Andi studied Bex's face. "How can you not be completely psyched about this? It could be the mother-daughter adventure of a lifetime!"

Bex crinkled her nose. "It *could*. But it's a pretty long drive on steep, winding mountain roads. . . ."

"Cool!" Andi couldn't think of anything better than taking a road trip with Bex on her motorcycle.

"And we would have to spend the *whole weekend* outside, except when we're asleep . . . in a *tent*."

"Sounds good to me," Andi insisted. She wasn't exactly the outdoorsy type, but going to Mountain Jam could be the perfect way to change that.

"But it can get pretty hot . . . and crowded . . . and dirty . . . and sweaty . . . and smelly," Bex continued.

Andi smiled with gritted teeth; she could handle a little heat and dirt.

"Plus, we would need to get a camping spot and tickets, and it's probably already sold out—"

"Um, hello?" Andi cut Bex off. "The Renaissance Boys are headlining! Bowie can get us in!"

Had Bex seriously forgotten? Right around the time Bowie had found out he was Andi's father, he was a touring guitarist with the Renaissance Boys. Of course, even though it had been his dream gig, he eventually decided to leave life on the road—mostly so he would be able to spend more time with Andi . . . and Bex. And although he'd opted to stick around Shadyside and get a job working at the local nursery, Andi figured he must still have some pull with the band.

"Maybe," Bex said with a reluctant sigh. "But I'm worried this might be more of an adventure than you're ready for."

"But, *Mo-om*," Andi whined, instantly making Bex flash back to all those times when *she* had been a teenager desperate to experience life, and *her* mom had kept trying to hold her back, telling her to slow down, to be more careful, to all but run away from anything even containing the letters *f*, *u*, and *n*.

Oh, no! NO! Bex's thoughts exploded in a silent terrified scream. *Have I turned into the fun police, just like CeCe? Is this what happens when you work too hard at becoming a responsible parent? Do you suddenly have to hand in your cool card, without even realizing it's happening? Is that what happened when CeCe had me? Is that what's happening now that I have Andi?*

"Okay, we'll ask him!" Bex swiftly changed her tune. She would *not* turn into her mother. The mere thought of it made her stomach turn. But then, before she could stop the words from escaping, she added a cautionary and extremely maternal "Just don't get your hopes up."

"Too late!" Andi told her. Andi shivered with anticipation as she pulled Bex into the Spoon; she couldn't wait to grab a table and start planning their trip.

Chapter 3

"Oh, hey, look who it is!" Bex glanced toward the counter as she and Andi sat opposite each other in one of the turquoise-and-orange booths.

When Andi spun around to see, her heart skipped a beat. It was Jonah Beck. As if he sensed her presence, he turned and waved the moment Andi looked his way. Andi felt her stomach do a little somersault at the sight of his sparkling green eyes and his adorable dimples. She couldn't help it. No matter how much they'd been through, first as friends, then as an item—or at least, in Andi's limited experience, what she *thought* had been an item—he still had a strange power over her.

"I'm gonna go over real quick," Andi told Bex, sliding out of the booth. "Can you order me a chocolate shake and some baby taters?"

"Sure—take your time!" Bex replied.

Andi went to sit down on the stool next to Jonah's. "Hey," she said.

"Hey!" Jonah smiled and nodded, causing his thick brown hair to flop down into his eyes.

"Are you here by yourself?" Andi asked.

"Yeah," Jonah said. "I was out skateboarding with some buddies and then I got *really* hungry, but they all had to take off. Baby tater?"

Andi looked down at Jonah's plate of half-eaten food and shook her head. "Oh . . . that's okay. I think Bex is already ordering some for me."

"Cool." Jonah checked his watch. "Whoa!"

"What?"

"I didn't realize how late it was!"

"I know, right?" Andi smiled, realizing that she felt kind of edgy being out so late on a Friday night.

"But . . . what are you doing here?" Jonah asked, looking confused.

Andi scowled. "What am *I* doing here? What are *you* doing here?"

"I told you—I was out skateboarding and got hungry."

"Well, Bex and I just went to the movies and then *we* got hungry." Andi challenged Jonah with her dark eyes.

"Yeah, but . . . it's *so late*," he said. "I mean, I didn't think you were the kind of person who would go out this late on a Friday night."

"Oh, really?" Andi's hands involuntarily clenched into fists. "What kind of a person *am* I, then?"

"I don't know." Jonah shrugged, his eyes darting around like he was searching for an escape route. "I guess I just think of you as pretty predictable—like you almost always come here on the same days, at the same hours, and you're almost always with Buffy and Cyrus. . . ."

Jonah trailed off and blinked a few times. He looked like a sad puppy dog. She knew he didn't mean it as an insult. But the more Andi thought about what he had said, the more upset she got.

"So by 'predictable,' you mean . . . 'boring,' right?" she finally asked through gritted teeth.

"Huh? No!" Jonah insisted. "I just meant that you're, um, *reliable*! I meant it in a good way. You're the kind of person I can totally count on, no matter what. It's one of the things I like best about you, Andiman."

Ugh. Sometimes Andi liked that Jonah called her by the nickname that had previously only been used by Bex, but right then she could tell he was using it to manipulate her into accepting his lame explanation. *Especially* when he punctuated it with his toothpaste-commercial-worthy smile and batted his long lashes. He wasn't going to charm his way out of this one.

"You say 'reliable,' but you *mean* 'boring,'" Andi muttered under her breath. "And why would you bother being friends with someone so predictable, so lacking in spontaneity, so *boooring*—"

"You're *not* boring! You're—" Suddenly, without warning, in an almost exact replay of what had happened to Andi earlier, Jonah's mouth fell open in a yawn, and he tried to hide it with his hands. But the damage was already done.

Oh my gosh, Andi thought. *I really* am *boring! Why else would Jonah be yawning?*

She cleared her throat. "I'd better get back to Bex," she whispered, sliding off her stool. But when she got back to the booth, she discovered Bex had set her head down on the table and was literally *snoring*!

Andi gasped. Jonah was yawning in her face, Bex was falling asleep when they were supposed to be out having fun, and she had just been accused of being *predictable*, which obviously meant *boring*.

"Wake up!" Andi shook Bex's shoulder a bit harder than she'd intended.

"What? Huh? Where are we?" Bex asked, rubbing her eyes and sitting up. "Oh, hey!"

"Hey!" Andi replied tersely. "So, come on, we need to start planning this road trip!"

"Whoa, slow down." Bex stretched her arms and yawned. "We need to make sure Bowie can get us tickets first."

"He can," Andi said. "He *has* to."

Andi had decided that even if Bowie couldn't make it happen, she would find a way to get to Mountain Jam—not only because it would be the trip of a lifetime, but because it was the most unpredictable thing she could think of doing.

Just wait until Jonah finds out I'm going to Mountain Jam! she thought as she stuck a straw into her shake and took a bigger gulp than she normally did. *We'll see what kind of a person he thinks I am* then!

Chapter 4

"Wow . . . isn't this fun?" Bex's voice was laced with sarcasm as she passed a platter of pancakes to Andi.

Andi and Bex had been invited over to CeCe and Ham's house for Saturday brunch—but the moment they arrived, CeCe commented on how exhausted they both looked. Now she was demanding to know *why* they were so tired. More specifically, she was drilling Bex on how strict she was about enforcing Andi's bedtime.

"I'm *serious*," CeCe said, shaking her glossy black bob. "What time does Andi go to bed?"

"Mom. It's the weekend. And she's thirteen." Bex rolled her eyes and stabbed her fork into a syrup-soaked pancake.

"People don't suddenly stop needing sleep when they hit their teens or the week draws to a close!" CeCe huffed.

"In fact, the National Sleep Foundation says children aged six to *thirteen* require between nine and eleven hours of sleep per night!"

Bex glared at her mother. "How do you even *know* that?"

"Because as a responsible parent, I stay on top of the latest research relating to childcare. Don't you?"

"Um, yeah!" Bex said, her raspy voice cracking. "But I'm not a child anymore . . . remember? I'm a responsible parent, just like you."

"Prove it," CeCe retorted. "What time did Andi go to sleep last night?"

Andi and Bex exchanged nervous glances.

"Well?" CeCe pressed, taking a sip of her tea.

"Hmmm . . . let's see." Bex looked at the ceiling and thought back to the previous night's activities. "We decided to go to the movies, but the earlier show was sold out, so ours ended at about eleven o'clock, and then we went to the Spoon . . . and then we went home . . . so I guess it was about midnight? Maybe twelve-thirty?"

CeCe nearly choked on her tea. "And what time did she get up this morning?"

"About eight," Andi volunteered without thinking.

"But only because you called so early to invite us over!" Bex shot an accusatory look at CeCe.

"Oh, I see—so it's *my* fault?" CeCe growled, staring at her bowl of muesli. Even though the rest of the family was having pancakes, eggs, and bacon, she maintained a strict diet that always began with muesli in the morning.

"No. It's *my* fault," Andi said, frowning as Bex and CeCe both turned to look at her. "I'm responsible for when I go to bed and when I wake up, and *I'm* the one who decided we should go to the movies. Bex wanted to stay home and rest."

"She *did*?" CeCe raised an eyebrow.

"Yes!" Andi insisted.

"It's true," Bex admitted sheepishly. "And now she's even trying to convince me to take her to Mountain Jam next weekend."

"*What?*" All the color drained out of CeCe's face.

"Yup—she's *my* kid, all right." Bex arched her dark eyebrows and flashed a smile.

"Well, you're not going to take her!" CeCe stood up. "Absolutely not."

"Um . . . it's not your decision to make, Mom." Sure, Bex still had some concerns about taking Andi to Mountain Jam, but she had many more concerns about letting CeCe dictate where they could or could not go.

"She's only thirteen, Rebecca," CeCe snapped. "How can you even think about taking her to *that place* . . . driving on *those roads* . . . spending an entire weekend with *those people*?"

Andi widened her eyes and waited to see what Bex would say next. A tiny part of her even wondered if she should have taken Bex more seriously when she said that Mountain Jam might be more of an adventure than Andi could handle.

"Why are you so concerned about *that place* . . . and *those roads* . . . and *those people*?" Andi asked, genuinely curious.

"It's like I told you," Bex cut in with a groan. "It's a

long drive on winding mountain roads, and it can get hot and crowded and dirty and sweaty and smelly, and you have to sleep in a tent, and blah, blah, blah."

"You told her all that?" CeCe's lips stretched into a tight smile.

"Yeah. And she still wants to go."

CeCe's smile withered, and she turned to look at Ham. "Are *you* going to say anything about this?"

"Oh, sure. Why not?" Ham's ruddy face broke into a grin, and his blue eyes sparkled. "It sounds like a pretty great time to me!"

"Hmmph." CeCe tugged down the hem of her crisp red cardigan. Then she grabbed her bowl from the table and marched into the kitchen without saying another word.

Chapter 5

"*Here, why don't you let me clean up?*" Andi offered, carrying her plate into the kitchen, where CeCe was dumping the soggy remains of her muesli down the sink.

"And me too," Ham added, walking into the kitchen with a few more dishes.

"Fine—but your doing the dishes isn't going to make me change my mind about you going to that place!" CeCe spun around and marched away.

"Wow." Andi looked at Ham and they exchanged the cringe of mutual amusement they'd perfected through the years.

"Yeah." Ham chuckled and began rinsing the plates. "Hurricane CeCe strikes again."

After they had done the dishes in silence for a few

minutes, Andi finally turned to Ham and asked, "So how much do you know about the music festivals Bex has gone to? I mean, what do *you* think Mountain Jam would be like?"

Instead of answering, Ham asked his own questions: "What do *you* think it would be like, and why do you want to go so badly?"

Andi thought for a minute. "Well, I kind of figured it would be a great mother-daughter adventure . . . and honestly?"

"Yes?" Ham dried his hands on his navy-blue button-down shirt.

"I figured that life with Bex as my mom would be a *nonstop* adventure," Andi said. "But lately, things seem like they're becoming kind of . . . boring. I'm even starting to think it might be my fault!"

"What?" Ham shook his head and laughed. "There's no way life with you—*or* Bex—could ever be boring."

Andi shrugged. "I don't know about that. . . ."

"But I guess I can kind of relate to what you're saying," Ham added.

"You *can*?"

"I can. The truth is there have been plenty of times when I've wondered if being married to me has made *CeCe's* life kind of boring."

"That's crazy!" Andi insisted, then lowered her voice to a whisper. "I mean, *you're* the fun one. CeCe is the . . . um . . . *you know*."

Ham nodded and gave Andi a quick wink. "There's a lot you don't know about your . . . CeCe. In fact, you've just given me a pretty great idea!"

"I have?" Andi smiled. "What is it?"

But before Ham could answer, there was a loud crash in the dining room.

"What was *that*?" Ham looked at Andi, and they both raced out of the kitchen only to find Bex and CeCe arguing—and a broken plate on the floor.

"Now look what you did!" CeCe barked.

"I didn't mean to drop it," Bex snapped back.

"You never *mean* for anything to go wrong," CeCe said, throwing up her hands. "It just *happens*."

"That's not fair—and it's not true!" Bex shouted, shaking her hands the exact way CeCe had.

CeCe stared at the ground. "I'm sorry," she said softly. "That didn't come out right. My point is that accidents can happen—especially on road trips and at music festivals. That's why I can't stand the idea of you taking Andi to Mountain Jam."

"But she'll be safe with me," Bex whispered.

"Will she?" CeCe challenged Bex with her eyes.

As Andi looked from Bex to CeCe, then back to Bex, Ham got a dustpan and brush out of the hall closet and began sweeping up bits of broken china.

"*Mom?*" Andi finally said, breaking the long silence.

"Yes?" Bex and CeCe replied in unison, eyes still fixed on each other.

Bex's jaw dropped and her eyes widened at CeCe. "She meant *me!*"

"Oh." CeCe cleared her throat.

"Yes?" Bex repeated, turning to look at Andi.

"Maybe we *shouldn't* go to Mountain Jam." Andi didn't

want to give up so easily, but she couldn't stand that it was creating so much tension between Bex and CeCe—not to mention that CeCe seemed genuinely worried something might go wrong. What if something *did* go wrong?

"Huh?" Ham glanced up at Andi, clearly surprised that she would change her mind so quickly after the conversation they'd had in the kitchen.

"Really?" CeCe's eyes lit up, and she pressed her hands together, bringing them to her lips as she looked gratefully at Andi.

But before Andi could reply, Bex grabbed her hand and marched toward the door. "Oh, we're going to Mountain Jam! We're going to talk to Bowie about getting us those tickets *right now*—and *nobody* is going to stop us!"

Bex tossed a defiant look at CeCe before flinging open the door and pulling Andi outside.

Chapter 6

When Bex and Andi arrived at Judy's Blooms, the nursery where Bowie worked, they found him elbow-deep in a flower bed full of pink and white tulips. His dark chin-length curls were pulled away from his face with a long red scarf, and he wore a dirt-covered purple apron with I'M ALL THUMBS—*GREEN* THUMBS! emblazoned across the front.

"That's quite an outfit you're wearing," Bex said with a smirk as she and Andi stood over him.

"Heyyy!" Bowie looked up, a goofy grin spreading across his face the moment he set eyes on Bex and Andi. "What's the haps, Macks?"

Bex cut right to the chase: "We were wondering if you still talk to any of the Renaissance Boys."

"It's nice to see you, too, Bex." Bowie tilted his head

and pouted. But then he laughed and flung his arms wide, pulling Bex into a big dirty hug before turning to Andi and covering her in potting soil, too.

Andi laughed and shook the dirt from her peach-colored shorts before giving Bex's plaid flannel shirt a brush-down.

"Sorry." Bex rewound and started again with Bowie. "How are things? How's the landscaper life treating you?"

"It's *awesome!*" Bowie put a grimy finger to his lips and said, "Shhh," then motioned for Bex and Andi to follow him as he literally tiptoed through the tulips to a big glass greenhouse. Inside were rows upon rows of stunning orchids—white ones, purple ones, yellow ones, white with yellow spots, yellow with purple spots, big ones, small ones, some arranged with leafy green plants and others with lucky bamboo.

"Wow!" Andi gasped, unsure where to look first. "Did you grow all of these?"

"I did!" Bowie said. "And I even named them all."

"*All* of them?" Bex laughed and whispered to Andi, "I think someone needs to get out more. . . ."

Bowie took Bex and Andi down each row of plants, introducing them to every one. "This little guy's named Buddy. Get it? *Bud?* And here we have Stan—short for Stanhopea, of course. Then these little ladies are Leilani, Puanani, and Moana. . . . Oh, and of course the most beautiful ones are Bex and Andi."

"Awww." Andi and Bex both laughed as the tour continued. When they got to the end of the meet and greet, Bex asked, "What on earth are you going to do with all of these?"

"Well, most of them are going to be hanging out in the VIP tents at the Mountain Jam fest next weekend," Bowie revealed.

Stunned, Andi and Bex whipped their heads around to stare at each other.

"It's a sign—from the universe!" Andi said in a hushed tone.

"*What's* a sign?" Bowie crinkled his nose.

"We just came here to ask you about Mountain Jam— to see if you might be able to ask the Renaissance Boys to get us tickets," Bex explained.

"Ohhh!" Bowie said. "Hence your question about me keeping in touch with them earlier."

"Uh-huh," Bex said. "We saw a poster for the festival last night, and Andi decided that our lives have become dull as . . . uh . . . *dirt*? So she's convinced that a music festival will cure us!"

Bowie smiled. "I see. . . . The apple doesn't fall far from the tree, does it?"

"Nope!" Bex grinned. "Try as I might—and try as *CeCe* might—to warn her against it, once the girl sets her mind on something—"

"Hey," Andi interjected, "I *did* say that maybe you and CeCe were right to be concerned and that maybe we shouldn't go."

"Ah!" Bex nodded. "But by then, I had already set *my* mind on going—or at least going against whatever CeCe tells me I should do. Or shouldn't do? Whatever."

Bowie gave his head a super-quick shake, like a dog does after getting out of water. "Okay, okay, I *think* I see where you're going with all this, but I haven't talked to any of the boys in the band in a while."

"Oh." Bex frowned.

"*However*," Bowie continued, "I can do even better than talking to them about getting you tickets."

"You can?" Andi widened her eyes.

"Yup! Since Judy's Blooms will be providing all these plants for the VIP tents, the event organizer sent us some VIP passes and even hooked us up with primo campsites. So consider yourselves to be *my* very important people."

"*VIP passes?*" Andi squealed. "That's *amazing!*"

"I know, right?" Bowie smiled. "Who would have thought I'd still get the rock-star treatment without even being an actual rock star?"

Andi studied Bowie's face, detecting a hint of melancholy in his expression. "Is it going to be weird to be there as, um, a flower man instead of a Renaissance *Boy*?" she asked tentatively.

"Nah!" Bowie insisted, leading Andi and Bex out of the greenhouse and to the front of the nursery. "I'm not interested in the band thing anymore. I have my girls and my plants and my sod and . . ."

Bowie kept talking, but his words were drowned out

by the screech of tires as a beat-up old truck pulled into the parking lot.

"What?" Andi shouted.

"I have my *rocks*. Check it out!" Bowie yelled, pointing at the truck. Piled in the back were boulders in every imaginable shape and size—and the name written on the doors was Rock-Star Landscape Design.

"See?" Bowie grinned. "I can even still be a rock star if I want!"

"Ha!" Andi smiled. But the longer she examined Bowie's expression, the more convinced she became that he wasn't quite as content as he wanted her to believe. In fact, she sometimes noticed that his left eye twitched when he was trying to hide something from her, and it was kind of doing that right then.

Did he miss the life he'd left behind when he found out that he had a daughter? He couldn't possibly think that hanging out with Andi and Bex in Shadyside or working at Judy's Blooms was more exciting than playing guitar with the Renaissance Boys . . . could he? Nope. No matter how much he might claim otherwise, Andi couldn't shake the feeling—once again—that she was responsible for a formerly free-spirited, totally adventurous person's completely average and seriously snooze-worthy life.

But at least they had Mountain Jam the next weekend to look forward to. Yes! At least they had that.

Chapter 7

After locking up her electric scooter at the school bike rack on Monday morning, Andi found Buffy and Cyrus sitting at one of the blue metal tables on the front quad.

"Hey, guys!" She slid her neon-green backpack off her shoulder and sat on the bench next to Buffy. "How was your weekend?"

Before either of them could respond, Jonah walked up. "Hey, guys!" He smiled at Cyrus and Buffy and then glanced tentatively at Andi. "How was your weekend?"

Cyrus and Buffy exchanged amused looks.

"What? What'd I say?" Jonah asked.

"The exact same thing Andi said precisely twelve point three seconds ago," Cyrus noted, checking his watch and then going into hyper-analytical mode. "Apparently, you both possess a sincere interest in how Buffy and I spend our extracurricular time . . . *or* you both struggle with post-weekend academic reentry and the conversational abilities required thereof."

"Huh?" Andi and Jonah said, crinkling their noses and tilting their heads at the same time.

"Fascinating!" Cyrus looked Andi up and down and then studied Jonah. "It's like you're one person inhabiting two bodies!"

Andi and Jonah laughed—again at the same time.

"See? You can't stop!" Cyrus seemed genuinely impressed but then shrugged it off. "Nah. I guess we all struggle with such things."

"*What* things?" Buffy widened her eyes at Cyrus.

"You know, going from all that downtime—*chillaxing with the peeps*," Cyrus said, doing his best hip-hop-star impression, before continuing in a stuffy tone, "to the more structured habits and behaviors demanded of public learning facilities."

"Uh-huh." Buffy laughed, then turned to look at Andi. "Anyway, how was *your* weekend?"

"So great!" Andi flashed a huge self-satisfied smile at Jonah. This was her chance to show him how unpredictable she could be. "I found out that Bowie is getting VIP passes for Mountain Jam next weekend, so Bex and I are going to go!"

Jonah's eyes practically doubled in size. "Whoa! That's awesome! I'm going, too."

"You are?" Andi asked, though she wasn't entirely surprised. Jonah always seemed to be going to the coolest places, trying out the latest things—like that time he'd discovered the new virtual reality arcade in town before anyone else. Andi still felt kind of bad about laughing at him when he got too into one of the games and fell down, seriously injuring his chin. Thank goodness he'd forgiven her for that.

"Yeah!" Jonah said. "My cousin Mona spends an insane amount of time trying to win tickets on the radio, and it totally paid off again this year."

"Jonah . . . and Mona?" Cyrus interjected. "That's even crazier than Cyrus . . . and Iris."

"Yeah, and we have an aunt Fiona." Jonah shrugged.

"Anyway, I'll never forget how much fun Mona and I had at Mountain Jam last year, even though she's older and into totally different things than I am. I can't wait to go again!"

Andi couldn't decide whether to be excited or irritated. She'd been wanting to impress her friends—especially Jonah—with the news that she was doing something none of them had ever done before. Something *super* unpredictable. But once again, Jonah had gotten there first.

"I've never been in the VIP area, though," Jonah continued, making Andi feel slightly better. "That would be *beyond* fun. Do you think Bowie could get any extra passes for me and Mona?"

Andi shrugged. "I'm not sure. But I guess I could text him and find out."

"That would be amazing. Thanks!" Jonah smiled so the dimples in his cheeks became more pronounced.

Andi turned to look at Buffy and Cyrus, who had been awfully quiet the whole time. "So what do you guys think? Can you believe I'm going on a road trip with Bex? On a motorcycle? To Mountain Jam?" Andi was determined to emphasize precisely how many unprecedented, adventurous, totally unpredictable things she would soon be doing.

"No, I really can't." Buffy did seem pretty shocked.

"I mean, obviously CeCe was completely against it," Andi continued. "She was going on and on about how dangerous it would be, driving on *those roads* and hanging out at *that place* with *those people*. Even Bex seemed a little unsure, at least until CeCe told us she didn't want us to go. Then it was like Bex and I were leading our own personal fight-the-power rebellion."

"Cool," Cyrus mumbled, apparently stunned into a rare moment of near silence.

"*Totally* cool," Jonah agreed. "I can't even imagine driving up there on a motorcycle. There are some gnarly switchbacks on the way up! And CeCe is kind of right about the place and the people, too. I mean, you should see how crowded the first aid tent gets. It's like some people make really bad choices when they go to music festivals, you know?"

Now, instead of being happy about what a thrill-seeking, *non*-boring person she must finally seem to Jonah, Andi got that sinking feeling again and worried that maybe the road trip *would* be more of an adventure than she was ready for. Or was Jonah kidding? Were there really that many people in need of first aid—and if so, why? What sorts of brainless things did people do at music festivals?

Andi wanted to grill Jonah on the details, but before she could, the warning bell for first period rang. So she grabbed her backpack and waved goodbye to her friends.

Her questions would have to wait until later.

Chapter 8

After her final class of the day, Andi headed for her locker to grab some books and then turned around to look for Buffy and Cyrus. But for some reason, they weren't at their lockers like they usually were. Andi was beginning to wonder if something was wrong. She hadn't seen them at their usual table for lunch, either, and they hadn't replied to her text messages asking where they were. As she scanned the hallway, her eyes bouncing from one crowd of kids to another, she pulled out her phone. But before she had a chance to send them yet another text, she saw them making their way toward the glass doors at the front of the building.

"Buffy! Cyrus!" Andi called out, swinging her backpack onto her shoulder and jogging after them.

Apparently, Buffy didn't hear her, because she kept

walking—but Cyrus glanced back. Then, with a panicked look in his eyes, he grabbed Buffy and shuttled her outside. Now Andi was super confused. She picked up her pace and finally managed to catch up to her friends near the bike rack where her scooter was locked.

"What's going on?" Andi asked when Buffy and Cyrus turned to face her. "Are you guys avoiding me or something?"

Cyrus was about to respond, but Buffy glared at him and shook her dark curls, warning him to stay silent.

"Buffy?" Andi searched her friend's face for some sort of clue but then turned to lock eyes with Cyrus, who tended to be an easier target when it came to extracting information.

Sure enough, Cyrus couldn't stay quiet, no matter how hard Buffy dug her nails into the material of his pale blue cardigan. "We're very disappointed in you, Andi Mack," Cyrus blurted out. "We always said we would all go to Mountain Jam together—you, me, and Buffy—after we all turned sixteen. But now you've decided to go with Bex instead . . . *three full years ahead of schedule!*"

Andi squinted, the details of that conversation slowly coming back to her. She had gotten so caught up in the excitement of planning her adventure with Bex that the stuff she'd discussed with her friends had obviously slipped her mind.

"Don't you remember?" Cyrus crossed his arms and raised a dark eyebrow, doing his best impression of a disappointed parent.

"Um . . . kind of?" Andi finally said. "But not really?"

"Seriously?" Buffy demanded, her eyes widening furiously. "How can you not remember? We talked about it for like a week straight! We said we would drive together in your future VW van and you and I were going to get matching henna tattoos!"

"We *were*?" Andi chewed on her lower lip. She did remember now that they reminded her, and she felt bad. But she decided it would be better to play dumb. "It's not . . . really . . . ringing . . . a bell. Maybe you guys made those plans without me?"

Beyond annoyed, Buffy tossed up her hands. Meanwhile,

Cyrus took a step closer to Andi and stared intently into her eyes. "You are *lying*, Andi Mack!" he declared.

"What?" Andi took a step backward. "N-no I'm not!"

"Yes, you are." Cyrus said. "Each of my parents has that special therapist-style way of knowing when someone isn't being truthful, and—call it nature or nurture—I realized early on that I, too, have the gift."

Andi thought fast. "Well, I can do the same thing with Bowie. His eye gets all twitchy when he's trying to hide something. So, well, I can't possibly be lying, because my eye isn't twitching, and, you know, it's got to be a genetic thing. Right?"

As Andi wove her way through the argument, her voice started to tremble.

"Aha!" Cyrus pointed directly into Andi's face. "The shaky voice never lies . . . or, well, the shaky voice *does* lie."

"You can't be serious!" Andi tried to laugh, but now she felt like she was on trial.

"Look, there are several key signs that someone is

lying, and I happen to know all of them," Cyrus said, pulling a pen from his pocket and waving it around as he launched into a point-by-point explanation while pacing in front of the bike rack. "The evidence may include, but is not limited to, chewing on the lower lip, a shaky voice, a twitchy eye—I'm impressed by you for observing that one with Bowie!—as well as tugging on the hair, sweaty palms . . . Those are the top five, but the list goes on from there."

"That's crazy." Andi shoved her hands into the pockets of her pants but then instantly removed them in case shoving hands into pockets was yet another sign of lying.

"No, it's quite common, actually," Cyrus retorted. "Sweat of the palm is the most difficult one to detect, unless you're as blessed with the gift as I am. But bottom line? You. Are. *Lying!*"

Andi looked from Cyrus to Buffy, whose face was getting flushed. "I can't believe this!" Buffy snapped. "First you forget our plans, and then you *lie* about the fact that you forgot them?"

"Not cool!" Cyrus added, trying to match Buffy's tone as she dragged him away, leaving Andi all alone.

Andi felt tears stinging her eyes. She couldn't remember a time when her friends had been that upset with her—and she couldn't entirely blame them.

"Hey, Andiman!"

Before Andi could process the situation any further, she turned to see Jonah approaching in his purple tie-dyed Space Otters T-shirt. "Oh . . . hey, Jonah," she said softly, blinking back her tears.

Seeing Jonah standing there, Andi remembered their conversation about Mountain Jam earlier—specifically, that she had agreed to ask Bowie about VIP passes for Jonah and his cousin. That was when inspiration hit: What if she asked Bowie to get tickets for Buffy and Cyrus so they could all go to Mountain Jam together after all? It wasn't the exact plan they had made, but maybe presenting them with tickets would be enough to make them decide to forgive her.

It was worth a shot!

Chapter 9

"So, I still can't get over the fact that you're going to Mountain Jam!" Jonah said as Andi pulled out her phone and sent a quick text to Bowie, asking if there was any way he could get a couple of extra tickets or even VIP passes for the festival.

"Oh?" Andi frowned, partly because she was still reeling from what had just happened with Buffy and Cyrus, but also because Jonah seemed to be implying—once again—that Andi was a certain kind of person who only belonged in a certain kind of place at certain times of the day or night. "Because I'm usually so *predictable* or *reliable* or whatever?"

"Andi . . ." Jonah sighed. "I told you I didn't mean it the way you took it. Honestly, I can't stand unreliable people."

Andi shrugged and stared down at her phone just as Bowie's reply popped up on the screen: HEY KIDDO. NO CAN DO. ☹ PERKS FOR VENDORS ARE KIND OF LIMITED. Andi's heart sank.

"Well, then I guess you can't stand *me*!" she said.

"What do you mean?" Jonah asked.

"Bowie can't get any extra VIP passes for you . . . and he can't get tickets for Buffy and Cyrus, either. So I'm basically becoming less and less reliable by the minute."

"Oh," Jonah said. "I didn't know you were trying to get tickets for them."

"Yeah. I sort of forgot that we'd made plans to go to Mountain Jam together a while back, so now they're pretty mad at me for going with Bex. I thought maybe if Bowie could get them tickets, they wouldn't be so angry. But like I said . . . I'm totally and completely unreliable."

"Hmmm. Well, I think it was really cool of you to even try to hook up those passes—and maybe we can still hang at the festival. If, that is, you'd be willing to spend some time with a *non*-VIP."

Andi had to laugh. "Sure, that sounds good. Although

I *am* still wondering about some of that stuff you said earlier."

"How many times are you going to make me apologize?" Jonah asked. "I don't think being reliable is boring! I never said you were boring! I think you're the coolest, most spontaneous, most unreliable person I've ever met in my life!"

"Okay, okay, you might be taking that a little too far in the other direction now." Andi smiled. "Besides, I wasn't even talking about *that* stuff you said. I meant the stuff you were saying about Mountain Jam. Like were you serious about the first aid tent getting super crowded and all that?"

"Oh, totally," Jonah said. "It's crazy how many people forget to wear hats and sunscreen when it's as hot as it is up there, and the sun is beating down on you all day long. If you've never seen heatstroke, trust me: it gets pretty gnarly. Plus, people forget to drink enough water, so they get dehydrated and literally collapse. Also? There's this pizza-eating contest that gets super out of control, and some people wind up . . . well . . ."

"Seriously?" Andi said. "How out of control could a pizza-eating contest be?"

"*So* out of control!" Jonah insisted. "But honestly? I kind of have this dream about entering the contest myself."

"You do?"

"Yeah." Jonah leaned in close, like he was about to reveal one of his deepest, darkest secrets. "Ever since I started reading *Guinness World Records* when I was five, I always thought it would be the coolest thing ever to get in there for winning an eating contest—maybe pies, although there's one with hot dogs that's like the Super Bowl of food-eating contests. Only problem is that it's on Coney Island."

"That's kinda far."

"Yeah. I was going to enter the pizza-eating contest at Mountain Jam last year, but Mona wouldn't let me."

"What? Why?"

"She said she didn't want me to get sick, since my parents were trusting her to keep me safe."

"Well, Bex would *never* stop me from entering—so maybe I'll have to try it myself," Andi said. "After all, it's not like Bex and I haven't already had our fair share of pizza-eating contests!"

"Andi, that contest is way too intense. There's no way you're going to enter. I mean, next thing you're going to tell me is that you're going to try skydiving!"

As Jonah laughed at his own joke, Andi felt her mood turn dark again—and this time it had nothing to do with Cyrus and Buffy. This time it was 100 percent because Jonah obviously thought that she was the most boring person he'd ever met. The question was, how was she once and for all going to prove to him that he was wrong?

Chapter 10

By the time Andi got home from school, she had decided to stop worrying about what Jonah thought of her—at least for the moment. But now she was back to thinking about Buffy and Cyrus and how she could make things right with them.

"Hey!" Bex greeted Andi as she walked into the living room and dropped her backpack on the floor. "How was school?"

"Don't ask." Andi frowned and slumped into a green chair.

"Too late . . . I already did!" Bex quipped, but she quickly became serious when she realized that Andi was genuinely distressed.

"Do you want to talk about it?" Bex asked.

Andi shook her head and tugged at the frayed ends

of her pink-and-gray friendship bracelet, which she had made with Buffy when they'd had a sleepover a few weeks earlier. As she pulled on the embroidery thread, the knot came loose and sent the little wooden bead at the end flying to the floor. "Nooo!"

Bex ran over to pick up the bead and handed it back to Andi.

Andi sighed. "My friendship bracelet broke—which I guess is pretty fitting, considering that the friendship itself is also broken!"

"Uh-oh." Bex stood behind Andi's chair and ran her fingers through Andi's short black hair, being careful to avoid the two white barrettes that pinned back her bangs. "Would a scalp massage help?"

Andi closed her eyes and tried to relax, but it was no use. "I'm not sure that anything is going to help," she said, opening her eyes and hanging her head back to look up at Bex. "Buffy is really mad at me—Cyrus, too."

"How come?" Bex headed to the velvet sleeper sofa, which folded out into her bed at night. She grabbed a round purple throw pillow and hugged it to her chest as she sat down.

"I completely forgot that we had talked about going to Mountain Jam together a while back. We said we would go after we all turned sixteen," Andi explained. "So when I told them I was going with *you*, they felt like I had abandoned the plans we'd made."

Bex nodded and twirled one of the little silver charms hanging off her black leather choker. "Well, maybe you should stick to that plan and wait until you're sixteen. . . ."

Andi narrowed her eyes at Bex. Was she trying to get out of taking Andi? Was she still worried about something going wrong—and if so, why wasn't she being honest with Andi about that? Then again, why hadn't Andi been honest with Buffy and Cyrus earlier?

"The thing is," Andi continued, "it's not just that I forgot we had those plans, but I kind of lied about forgetting—like I said maybe I wasn't there when *they* made that plan."

"Oh." Bex continued to play with her necklace as she

considered what sort of advice to offer. "Well, there's only one way to fix that: you have to tell them the truth and apologize for lying."

"Then how about if you tell *me* the truth about Mountain Jam?" Andi replied. "Why have you been reluctant to take me? Are you worried about the same stuff as CeCe? Do you think I'm going to get hurt and wind up in the first aid tent or something?"

Bex tossed aside the purple pillow, got up from the couch, and began pacing. "Truth?" she finally said, looking into Andi's eyes.

"Truth!"

"I *am* a little worried about taking you there."

"But why?"

"It's a whole new level of responsibility," Bex explained. "All the other times I've been to music festivals like this, I've only had to worry about taking care of myself. Now I need—and I desperately *want*—to take care of you, too. I don't know what I would do if anything bad ever happened to you!"

"But what do you think is going to happen?"

"Hopefully nothing—but just in case, I've been putting together a safety-first kit!"

"Um. Okay . . . ?" Andi raised an eyebrow.

Bex grabbed a red bag from the corner of the room and started unpacking it, describing each item as she set it down on the couch: "Plenty of sunscreen and a huge hat, so you don't get burned. A refillable water bottle, so you don't get dehydrated. Tons of baby wipes, to keep the festival dirt, sweat, and grime to a minimum. A rain poncho, in case the weather takes a turn for the wet. Bug spray, so we don't get bitten. Bandannas, to protect our mouths and noses from mountain dust . . ."

Andi smiled. It was pretty sweet that Bex had already put so much thought into keeping her safe—plus, the floppy yellow hat was super cute.

"Also," Bex continued, "I'm putting a photocopy of my driver's license in here."

"Why?"

"I once read that it's always good to have a backup copy when you go on road trips, in case you lose the real one," Bex explained.

"Couldn't you just store a photo of it in your phone?"

"That's a great idea. I'll do that, too!" Bex smiled and quickly snapped a shot of her license, then put it back in her wallet.

"What about the VIP passes?" Andi asked. "Where are you keeping those?"

"They're right here," Bex said, opening her wallet again and letting two laminates dangle from purple lanyard strings. "I connected the strings to the key ring in my wallet, so they can't possibly fall out or get lost."

"Wow. You're pretty good at this whole responsible-mom thing."

"Thank you!" Bex grinned but then immediately frowned. "But a responsible mom doesn't mean a *boring* mom . . . right?"

"Right!" Andi agreed. "Just so you know, though, I'm already pretty responsible. I mean, I'm not going to leave my brain at home just because it's my first music festival ever."

Bex laughed. "Yeah. I know that."

"However," Andi added with a sly smile, "I *am*

thinking about entering the pizza-eating contest."

"Who told you about *that*?" Bex's eyes grew wide.

"Jonah," Andi replied. "He said it gets totally out of control—but I'm thinking, how out of control can it really be? To me, it just sounds . . . *intriguing? Awesome? Delicious?*"

"Andi." Bex got super serious. "I know it sounds awesome at first—but I swear, I didn't eat any pizza for an entire year after the competition."

"Wait . . . *you* entered the pizza-eating contest at Mountain Jam?"

"Um . . . have you met me?"

"*And* you didn't eat pizza for a *whole year*?" Andi wasn't sure which part was more shocking.

"Yeah, even though I only took home the third-place ribbon." Bex puffed out her lower lip in an exaggerated pout. "It's stuck somewhere near the bottom of my memory box."

"You sure are full of surprises, aren't you?" Andi laughed.

"See?" Bex smiled. "Responsible *and* unpredictable, all in one best-mom-ever package!"

Chapter 11

For the rest of the week, Andi struggled to balance her excitement about Mountain Jam with her guilt about the situation with Buffy and Cyrus. She had tried to talk to both of them—first via text, then on the phone, then at their lockers before school, then in the cafeteria, then after school in the quad. But each time Andi reached out, they shut her down, ignored her, or simply weren't available. Even Cyrus had mastered a certain aloofness Andi had never seen in him before.

So Andi shifted her focus to getting all her schoolwork out of the way and, of course, planning for the road trip and festival. Fortunately, Bex seemed to have finally let go of most of her concerns about taking Andi— especially when they started figuring out their wardrobe for the weekend. To start, Bex made sure that Andi had a solid pair of motorcycle boots, and she also found an awesome red leather moto jacket for her at Nine Lives, their favorite vintage shop in town. Then it was time to put together the perfect festival wear. That would require a full-on fashion show, Bex insisted, so that they could test-drive each option and rate it for both comfort and cuteness.

"What do you think?" Bex asked, strutting around the living room while Andi sat on the couch eating animal crackers.

"I love it!" Andi clapped, giving especially high marks to the crocheted white fringe top, which Bex had paired with denim cutoffs and suede booties. But it was the accessories—particularly the heavy silver-and-turquoise neckpiece—that really took the look to the next level. "Show me another one!"

"Okay!" Bex ducked into Andi's bedroom to change and emerged a few minutes later looking like a bohemian goddess in a jeweled tank top, leather vest, and tie-dyed maxi skirt.

"It's perfect," Andi gasped, scanning her mother from

head to toe and then back up to the top of her head again before squinting and reconsidering. "Just one minor adjustment . . ."

Andi got up and took one of the thicker silver chains from around Bex's neck. Then she went to grab some elastic, along with a handful of crystal beads and flowers, from the craft box in her bedroom. Moments later, she placed the newly fashioned headpiece on top of Bex's dark wavy hair. "*Now* it's perfect."

Bex went to look at herself in the mirror and nodded approvingly. "It really is. It's like a crown! Now you go."

Andi returned to her room and considered the various options strewn across her purple paisley comforter. First she grabbed a green off-the-shoulder peasant top with white embroidery, along with a pair of white denim jeans. She checked herself in the mirror and frowned. Just like with Bex's last outfit, she felt like something was missing—but what? She looked around her room until her eyes landed on the collection of scarves hanging on the white wicker headboard. *Yes!* She grabbed the one Bex had sent her from Mountain Jam a few years earlier and quickly fashioned it into a headband, checking herself in the mirror again. *Now* it was working.

"Gorgeous!" Bex proclaimed when Andi sashayed through the living room, swinging a strappy white satchel over her shoulder and striking different poses. "The scarf looks *awesome!*"

"Thank you." Andi bowed her head and then raced back into the bedroom to change into her next outfit: a gauzy yellow tunic decorated with red henna suns, moons, and Sanskrit lettering. It was just long enough to work as a minidress. For accessories, she traded the scarf in her hair for a headband with feathers and beads, which she had made from a gold dream catcher.

Bex's jaw dropped when Andi returned to the living room and spun around a few times. "Seriously? You're so good at this!" Then she narrowed her eyes and shot a sideways glance at Andi. "Are you *sure* you never snuck out and went to Mountain Jam without CeCe knowing?"

"Ha!" Andi shook her head. "I don't think I would have been able to sneak out to do something like that even if I were sixteen!"

The moment she said that, Andi's thoughts returned to Buffy and Cyrus and the plans they'd made, and her heart sank.

"What's up?" Bex asked, noticing the quick change in Andi's mood.

"I've been trying to apologize to Buffy and Cyrus all week, but they won't even talk to me or return my messages."

"Oh." Bex frowned. "That stinks."

"Tell me about it."

"Maybe you need to bribe them," Bex proposed, grabbing the box of animal crackers off the coffee table and popping a few into her mouth.

"Bribe them?" Andi grimaced.

"Well, not exactly *bribe* them," Bex said between chews. "But bring them some sort of peace offering."

Andi thought about it for a moment. "Actually, that's a great idea!"

After school on Friday, Andi knew exactly where she would find Buffy and Cyrus—unless they were going to avoid the Spoon to avoid Andi. Thanks to her electric scooter, she was able to get there quickly and set up everything in the hopes that they would show. Once it was all ready, she checked her watch and then checked the door. Sure enough, in they walked—right on time. Maybe there were some good things about being predictable after all.

"I come bearing gifts," Andi said as soon as Buffy and Cyrus settled in at their usual booth. With a flourish, she set down a tray piled high with baby taters along with two chocolate shakes with extra whipped cream.

Buffy looked like she was literally going to climb over the back of the booth to escape, but Andi sat down and draped an arm around her, creating a physical barrier so Buffy couldn't leave.

"Listen," Andi began, looking at Buffy and then across the table at Cyrus. "I know you guys don't want to hear it, but I really am sorry that I forgot about the plans we made to go to Mountain Jam together."

Buffy scooted toward the wall, putting as much distance as she could between her and Andi. But Andi could see that Cyrus was softening a bit. His big dark eyes peeked from under his wavy black hair, encouraging her to keep going.

"But I'm especially sorry for acting like I didn't remember all the details when you reminded me—because I did, and I do," Andi continued earnestly. "And honestly? It's not going to be nearly as fun going without you guys."

"But you're still going, right?" Buffy muttered under her breath.

Andi mashed her lips together. "I am . . . and I wish I could take you with me. I even asked Bowie if he could get more tickets so that I *could* take you."

"Really?" Cyrus's face lit up.

"Yeah, but he couldn't do it." Andi sighed. "I'm really, really, *really* sorry."

Cyrus glanced at Buffy and then reached across the table to give Andi's hand a squeeze. "I forgive you."

Andi's mouth dropped open. "You do?"

"You apologized, so . . . of course!" Cyrus made a little

clicking noise with his mouth and shot one of his trademark finger-gun-and-wink combos at Andi.

Andi smiled and turned to look at Buffy. "How about you?"

Buffy stared down at the baby taters and popped one into her mouth. Then she ate another. And another. Finally, after polishing off half the plate, along with most of her milkshake, Buffy looked at Andi. "Okay, fine. I forgive you."

"Are you sure?" Andi batted her lashes at Buffy. "You still seem kind of mad."

"I'm not mad in the least," Buffy insisted. "Totally over it. No big deal. Moving on."

Andi desperately wanted to believe her friend. But how could she, considering that Buffy's voice was totally shaking? What had Cyrus said about the various signs that people were lying? *The shaky voice never lies . . . or, well, the shaky voice* does *lie!*

On the bright side, Buffy's lie included forgiving Andi. So maybe, eventually, she really *would* forgive Andi. At least, Andi would try to believe as much.

Chapter 12

"So are you girls all ready for your trip tomorrow?"
Ham asked, raising his eyebrows as he looked across the
dining table at Andi and Bex.

CeCe had insisted on making them "one last home-
cooked meal" before they left, as if they would be heading
off to live in the wilderness for the next few months instead
of spending a couple of nights camping at a music festival.

"Definitely!" Andi said.

"I hope your sleeping bags are going to be warm
enough," CeCe said softly, and Andi could see tears well-
ing up in her eyes.

"They will, Mom," Bex insisted. "I got Andi the exact
same one that saw me through countless nights of camping, even in subzero temperatures."

CeCe frowned. "Well, *that's* encouraging."

"It *is* encouraging," Ham interjected, placing a hand gently on top of CeCe's. "Bex has been taking care of herself for a long time now, and she's done a pretty phenomenal job of it."

"This is different," CeCe said under her breath. "She's not just going to have to take care of herself this time—she's going to have to keep Andi safe, too. Aren't you the least bit worried about how she's going to do that?"

"I'm right here," Bex said through gritted teeth. Even though CeCe was basically echoing the exact concerns Bex had expressed to Andi, it still annoyed her. "I can hear every word you're saying—and though I wouldn't normally say this out loud, because I have something known as humility, I'm *great* at keeping Andi safe. I've actually been doing a pretty phenomenal job of it for several months now, if I do say so myself."

"I agree," Andi chimed in.

"Me too," Ham added.

"Thanks, you guys," Bex said before turning back to CeCe. "Look, I know where this is coming from. I know that you're worried—and to be completely honest, I've been a little worried, too. I know it's a huge responsibility, taking Andi with me on her first road trip to her first music festival. But please trust me. I'm going to make sure she's safe and protected and very, very warm. I need you to believe that."

CeCe nodded and wiped away the tears that had settled into the fine lines around her eyes. "I'm trying to, Rebecca. I really am."

"Well, that's something, I guess." Bex tried to smile.

"Would you please reconsider taking the car, though?" CeCe implored. "I would feel so much better if you would borrow it. I can't stand the idea of Andi riding on the back of that . . . that . . . *thing*."

Bex laughed. "It's called a *motorcycle*, Mom—and, again, it's seen me through *a lot*. In fact, I think it would be more dangerous if I tried to drive a car at this point. I'm way more comfortable riding a bike."

CeCe sighed and put up her hands. "Okay, fine. Let's just try to enjoy our last meal together, then."

Andi and Bex exchanged amused looks. CeCe was really going for full melodramatic effect.

"You're going to see us again!" Andi jumped up and went to wrap her arms around CeCe. "We'll be back on Monday, and we'll have *a lot* more meals together!"

"I know." CeCe blinked back a few more tears and grabbed Andi's hands, squeezing them tight. "At least, I hope so."

Andi laughed and shook her head. "Oh, CeCe."

After dinner, Andi went into the kitchen to help Ham finish cleaning up.

"Can I ask you something?" Andi said as she took a plate to the sink and started rinsing it.

"Anything!" Ham smiled.

"Why aren't you worried about me and Bex going on this trip in the same way that CeCe is worried?"

"That's a good question. I guess I just see the world in a slightly different way than your mom . . . er, *CeCe* does. She has this sort of sixth sense sometimes—or at least she likes to think she does, you know? She's a trouble-shooter, and so she tries to anticipate things that might go wrong, so she can fix them before they even happen."

Andi nodded. "How come you're not that way?"

Ham shrugged. "I *can* be, sometimes, but usually I'm more of a wait-and-see guy. That's not always good, either. It means I'm not always prepared for problems that might come up."

"Because you're so focused on everything that could go right?"

"Yeah, that's a good way to look at it. Of course, sometimes that means I get disappointed, but I also get to enjoy each moment as it happens. CeCe, on the other hand, expects the worst and then gets to be pleasantly surprised!"

"So which should I be?" Andi wondered.

"Well, I would hate for you to worry your way through this trip. I think Bex is a lot more responsible than CeCe sometimes realizes, and I know you'll be in good hands with her."

Andi grinned as she handed a plate to Ham. "Me too."

"Also," Ham added, his blue eyes lighting up, "I think CeCe tends to forget how much fun she used to have at these kinds of festivals."

Andi's jaw dropped. "Wait . . . has she been to Mountain Jam before?"

"No, not Mountain Jam," Ham said. "But we did go to our share of outdoor concerts and festivals and on camping trips—all that good stuff—back in the day."

"Really?"

"Really." Ham chuckled.

"Did anything go wrong? Is that why CeCe's so worried?"

"All I remember are the good times we had, especially at the very first music festival we went to together. It was incredible!" Ham shook his head and smiled, closing his eyes as his mind traveled back in time. "CeCe looked breathtaking! The bands we saw, the people we met . . . it was wild. I tell you, we made a ton of memories on that trip that I'll cherish forever."

Andi got goose bumps, picturing a young Ham and CeCe at some giant outdoor venue.

"You know what else?" Ham whispered, leaning in close. "I even asked Bowie if he might be able to get us a couple of tickets to Mountain Jam. But don't tell anyone—*especially* CeCe! I want it to be a surprise."

"Oh." Andi frowned. "That's so great, but I don't think

Bowie can get more passes. I already asked him if he might be able to get tickets for Buffy and Cyrus, and he said vendors don't get that many. I guess if he were still in the Renaissance Boys or something, it would be different."

"Ah, well," Ham replied. "I figured it was a long shot."

"I'm so sorry."

"Don't be! All the more reason for you to seize this moment and make the most of it. It's clearly the opportunity of a lifetime!"

Andi smiled. Ham was right. She was lucky to be going on this trip with Bex—*and* getting VIP passes! Like Ham, she needed to focus on everything that could go right and on making memories she would cherish forever, just like Ham and CeCe had at their first festival.

She could hardly wait.

Chapter 13

Bright and early on Saturday morning, Bex and Andi rushed through a quick breakfast, eager to get their bags onto the back of the bike and hit the road. Bex had explained to Andi that if they left any later than eight o'clock, they might not have time to get settled in their tent—and even though they were most looking forward to seeing the Renaissance Boys close out the festival on Sunday, they would *not* want to miss the first day's performances. "Especially since I will be going *the speed limit—and not a single digit over*—the entire ride, we need to give ourselves plenty of time to get there," Bex added, mimicking CeCe's clipped words as she quoted her mother's warning.

From the moment she strapped on her helmet and hopped onto the back of the bike, Andi could feel adrenaline kicking in—but only the good kind, not the nervous kind. She had taken Ham's words from the previous night to heart, and now, cruising out of Shadyside and beginning the climb up the mountain, she couldn't remember a time when she'd felt so free—so alive.

But then, as the roads got steeper and Bex slowly wound around the first switchback, and then another, and then another, Andi began to feel something else: *queasy*. She thought back to what CeCe had said about "those roads" and tightened her arms around Bex, who immediately sensed that something was wrong. As soon as they got to the next turnout, Bex guided the bike to a patchy grass area and turned off the engine.

"What's up?" Bex asked, pulling off her black helmet. "Are you feeling okay?"

Andi took off her own helmet, and a look of panic flashed across Bex's face. "Oh my gosh, Andi! You're so pale! Do you need some water?"

"I-I think I might be getting carsick . . . or, you know, bike-sick?" Andi clutched her stomach and glanced at the road, which seemed to be contorting into waves.

Bex went straight for her bag, pulling out the safety-first kit. After fishing around for a moment, she produced a bag of ginger candies and gave one to Andi. "Here, take this," Bex said, then added, "Good thing you mentioned the pizza-eating contest the other day, or I might not have packed this."

Andi cringed, her stomach lurching at the thought of eating the candy. But she knew that without it, her stomach would be churning even more—and there was no way she was going to let anything ruin their trip.

"These roads can be pretty tough on the stomach," Bex noted sympathetically, "but we're through the worst of it. Don't worry—you'll be feeling better in no time."

"Thanks." Andi smiled weakly, taking deep breaths while Bex rubbed her back.

After about ten minutes, the queasiness began to subside, and Andi told Bex she was ready to get back on the road.

"You sure?" Bex ran a hand over Andi's cheek. "You *are* getting some color back."

"Then let's do this," Andi insisted.

Luckily, Bex had been right. There weren't nearly as many twists and turns as they continued their drive up the mountain, and the ginger candy had definitely helped soothe Andi's stomach. At last, she felt like she could relax and enjoy the ride again.

But that was when things took a different kind of turn. Even though the road was completely straight, the bike suddenly skidded, and once again, Andi's thoughts flashed back to CeCe talking about "those roads." Then Bex lost control of the bike and Andi heard her scream. Andi screamed, too, and her life started to flash before her eyes as the bike continued to skid toward the side of the road.

As Bex struggled to recover, the bike finally slid to a stop mere inches from the edge of the mountain.

"You okay? You okay?" Bex asked once they both had their boots safe on solid ground. She grabbed Andi's shoulders and stared into her eyes.

"Uh-huh," Andi said, still shaking. "Are you?"

"Yeah." Bex pulled off her helmet and crouched down to inspect the motorcycle. "But unfortunately, this tire is not."

"What?" Andi gasped, squatting down to get a better look. "Oh, no! Is it flat?"

"It sure is."

Andi glanced at the side of the mountain, and her heart began to race when she realized how long the drop was.

"Bex, that was crazy! I seriously thought we were going to die. What if the bike had gone over that edge?"

Bex pulled Andi into a tight hug. "I don't even want to imagine that. I promised I would make sure you're safe and protected. I will *always* make sure of that."

"I know," Andi whispered, tears stinging her eyes. "I've just never been so terrified in my whole life."

"Me neither," Bex admitted. Then, smiling through her own tears, she added, "But, hey, you said you wanted an adventure, right? I think this pretty much tops the list for me! Who's bored *now*?"

"Not me!" Andi replied. "*Definitely* not me. But how are we going to get to the festival with a flat tire?"

Bex tilted her head and thought for a moment. Then her eyes lit up. "Manny!"

"Manny?"

"Yeah! He's an old biker friend of mine—and he has an auto shop just up the road. Or at least he used to."

"How are we going to get *there*, though?" Andi asked.

"We'll walk!"

"Seriously?" Andi groaned.

"Come on, kid—it's not *that* far," Bex insisted, steering the motorcycle onto the road. "Help me push this thing! Embrace the adventure!"

"Okay, okay." Andi grimaced as the words "be careful what you wish for" echoed in her head.

Chapter 14

After about ten minutes of helping Bex push the motorcycle uphill, with the sun beating down on them, Andi stopped.

"Are we there yet?" she whined.

Bex laughed and rolled her eyes. "It's just another mile or so."

"A *mile*? Ugh!"

Andi was seriously wondering if they were going to make it to the repair shop. She was trying to channel Ham's positive outlook, but walking on a steep incline in heavy motorcycle boots wasn't helping matters. Plus cars kept speeding by, and every so often someone would whoop or holler out the window at Bex and Andi. Maybe *that* was what CeCe had meant when she had worried about "those people" and "those roads."

"Yo!"

Great. Yet another person shouting at them from a window. Only this time, the person didn't just shout; he pulled over. Then three guys who looked about Bex's age got out of their silver four-door pickup truck and headed straight for Bex and Andi.

"Bex," Andi whispered. "What's going on? Should we ditch the motorcycle and run?"

"Stay here with the bike," Bex whispered back, and then she *did* run—not away from the guys, but directly toward them.

"Bex? Is it really you?" yelled the guy who had been driving, as Bex jumped into his arms and gave him a huge hug. He wore a white T-shirt with jeans and a black leather jacket and had chiseled features, along with dark slicked-back hair and sideburns. He kind of looked like one of those classic movie stars from the '50s—a lot like James Dean, actually.

Rebel Without a Cause! Andi suddenly thought.

But who was he really, and how did Bex know him?

"Andi, this is Jagger Simon." Bex grabbed the guy by

his arm and led him to where Andi was standing with the bike while his friends hung back and leaned against the side of the truck. "We went to high school together, but I haven't seen him in years!"

"Hey." Jagger nodded coolly in Andi's direction.

"Hey." Andi swallowed hard. It was *crazy* how much he looked like James Dean.

"Andi's my . . . daughter," Bex added.

"*What?* No way!" Now Jagger lunged for Andi and swept her up into a hug. "It's so cool to meet you."

"You too." Andi grinned.

Jagger turned and motioned at the guys leaning against the truck. "Those are my buddies Zane and Luke. We're on our way to Mountain Jam."

"So are we!" Bex said. "At least, we *will* be if we can get this flat tire fixed."

Jagger bent down to examine it. "Yikes, that looks bad. Why don't we give you a lift?"

"Yes!" Andi squealed before Bex could reply.

"I guess that's a yes." Bex laughed. "But you don't have to take us all the way up to the festival. I want to get this tire fixed, so we just need to get as far as the repair shop. It's only about another mile."

"You sure?" Jagger furrowed his brow.

"Absolutely!" Bex grabbed the bags off the back of the bike and let Jagger steer it to the truck, where his friends helped him lift it onto the bed before turning to be introduced to Bex and Andi.

Once they'd all met, Luke offered the front passenger seat to Bex and climbed into the back with Zane. Andi had to sit somewhat awkwardly between Luke and Zane, but it sure beat walking the rest of the way to the repair shop.

"Cozy!" Luke said, smiling at Andi and checking to make sure her seat belt was fastened. "You good?"

"Uh-huh, thanks." Andi smiled back. Luke sort of reminded her of Ham, with his sandy blond hair and blue eyes—although he had a much lankier frame. Zane looked like he could be part of the Mack family, too—except he had more Bex and Andi's coloring, with his black hair and dark eyes. Both of them wore the same sort of comfy clothes Bex usually favored—classic-rock band shirts beneath plaid flannel button-downs, along with distressed jeans.

"Mountain Jam! Whoo!" Zane shouted, pumping a fist out the back window. "Are you guys stoked or what?"

"Totally," Andi said. "It's my first time ever going to a music festival."

"That. Is. Awesome," Luke replied.

"Yeah, can you believe it's her first music festival ever *and* she's getting VIP passes?" Bex added, glancing back.

"Seriously? *So* awesome." Luke grinned at Andi and chewed on his lower lip, then whispered, "We have VIP passes, too."

Wait a minute . . . Andi's mind flashed back to that conversation she'd had with Cyrus, when he'd listed the top five signs that someone was lying. Hadn't he said one of the signs was *chewing on the lower lip*? Was Luke lying about having VIP passes? Why would he lie about something like that—and why wouldn't Jagger and Zane call him on it? Had they not heard him, since he'd said it so softly? Should Andi repeat what he'd said, louder, so they could confirm whether he was lying about it?

Stop worrying! Focus on all the good things that could happen! Andi told herself, trying to channel Ham's outlook again. *Who cares if he's lying about having passes? Maybe he just wishes they had VIP passes or he's trying to impress us or something. It's not a big deal.*

What *was* becoming a big deal, though, was how loudly Andi's stomach was growling.

"Whoa—was that your stomach, or are you smuggling a wolf under that jacket?" Luke asked, chuckling.

"Um." Andi was mortified. She tapped Bex's shoulder and leaned forward to whisper, "Do you have any food in your purse?"

Bex rifled around in her bag for a minute and then whispered back, "I don't. I'm sorry. I should have packed something, like a responsible mom! Why didn't I put food on my safety-first list?"

Andi's stomach growled even louder, and Luke not only laughed this time but growled back. It was so awkward!

"You don't even have some gum?" Andi whispered more urgently to Bex.

"Let me see."

Jagger was already pulling up to the repair shop by the time Bex located some breath mints stuck to the bottom of her wallet. She handed them to Andi. "Here—at least it's something."

Andi cringed at the lint-covered candies, but she was desperate, so she took them.

"I promise we'll stop and get some food as soon as we get the tire fixed, okay?" Bex added.

"Okay," Andi agreed, trying to come up with a positive spin on the situation—like, hey, she might starve to death, but she would have fresh breath.

It wasn't much . . . but as Bex had said, at least it was something.

Chapter 15

As soon as Jagger pulled up to the repair shop, a weathered-looking man with a gray beard and a red bandanna in his long silvery hair walked out of the garage. He wore navy-blue coveralls, and sure enough, the name "Manny" was embroidered in red thread on his upper left pocket.

"Bex?" Manny wiped his greasy palms on his coveralls and squinted in the sunlight. "That you?"

"Hey, Manny! It's so great to see you!" Bex went to him and draped an arm around his shoulders, then introduced him to Andi, along with Jagger, Luke, and Zane.

As the guys lifted the motorcycle out of the back of the truck, Bex explained the situation to Manny.

"Let's take a look," Manny said, checking out the tire. He reached down, ran his fingers over the rubber tread, stopped for a minute, and promptly produced a sharp, rusty nail. "And there it is!"

"Oh my gosh, I didn't even see that!" Bex examined the nail. "How could I have let this happen?"

"It's not something you *let* happen. It's simply something that *does* happen—a lot," Manny pointed out, stroking his beard. "And by the looks of it, this one happened a few weeks ago."

"Are you serious?" Bex sighed. "I should have had the tires checked before we even left."

"Now *that* may be true, but you're not the first person or the last to make a mistake like that," Manny insisted with a wink.

Andi agreed. "CeCe has gotten at least three flat tires from driving over nails in the past couple of years."

"Really?" Bex's mouth fell open. "I can't believe it! I was already anticipating all the awful things she was going to say to me about being irresponsible and endangering your life if she ever found out about this—but maybe I'm not such a bad mom after all."

"You're *not* a bad mom," Andi said just as her stomach

growled again. "Except . . . well, I *am* still kind of starving here."

"Oh! You've gotta try the Second Breakfast Diner. It's just around the corner from here," Manny told them. "Best burgers and onion rings on the mountain!"

"Perfect!" Bex replied. "Can you patch the tire while we go get something to eat?"

"You betcha."

"Thank you so much, Manny." Bex smiled. "We'll be back soon."

"Take yer time."

Bex turned to Jagger and thanked him for the ride, and they agreed to meet up again at Mountain Jam. Jagger entered his contact info into Bex's phone, and then, finally, Bex and Andi were on their way to the diner.

"I hope this won't make us super late to the festival," Andi said when they arrived at the Second Breakfast Diner. It didn't look like much: a small rustic wood cabin built into the side of the mountain, with a creaky arched door. But once they got inside, Andi could tell from all the delicious smells that they were definitely in for a good meal.

"Don't worry about it," Bex said with a sly smile. "I actually planned for possible delays, which is why we left at eight instead of ten."

"Seriously?" Andi shook her head and laughed as they sat down in a dark wood booth with a checkered red-and-white tablecloth. "Once again, full of surprises—and yet oh so responsible, too."

"You know it." Bex winked.

The moment they sat down, a woman slithered up beside them—almost like she had appeared from beneath the peanut-shell-covered floorboards—and set a couple of menus on the table.

"Welcome to the Sssecond Breakfassst," the woman said in a low, raspy voice. Her big watery blue eyes were sunken into her face, and she had wispy brown hair pulled back into a bun beneath her white waitress cap. She wore a light pink button-down dress with a frilly white collar and matching apron, and the name "Tara" was handwritten on a white name tag on her pocket. "You mussst try the ringsss!"

Bex stifled a laugh as she looked across the table at Andi. "The onion rings?" Bex smiled up at the waitress. "Yeah, we hear they're great."

"Oh, yesss, they are, my preciousss!" Tara said, like she was doing an impression of Gollum from *The Lord of the Rings*. Then, making the similarity even more pronounced, she looked at Bex's hand and declared, "Ohhh! That ring! You mussst tell me where you got that ring!"

Bex couldn't hold back any longer—she burst out laughing but then pretended it was because she thought the waitress was just joking about her turquoise ring. "Aw, this old thing? I've had it for years. I got it at a little roadside stand in Taos when I was passing through New Mexico."

"Ssso preciousss!" Tara seized Bex's hand and took a good long look at the ring before turning her attention back to Bex and Andi. "I'll be back to take your order in a moment!"

Bex and Andi gawked at each other after the waitress slithered away.

"That was crazy!" Bex whispered, grabbing a few peanuts from the silver bucket in the middle of the table, cracking them open, and tossing the shells on the ground—which was apparently expected at the place. "What a character!"

"Seriously," Andi agreed, taking a few peanuts herself. "As in a character from *Lord of the Rings*?"

"Yes!" Bex pressed her lips together so she wouldn't burst out laughing again. "And she's obsessed with rings, too! *My* ring . . . the *onion* rings!"

"She *is* the lord—or at least the lady of the rings!" Andi giggled and put on her best raspy voice as she grabbed Bex's hand and stared at her ring. "Ohhh, my preciousss! I mussst have it!"

Bex wiped the tears of laughter that were rolling down her cheeks, then sighed. "I can't believe how much has already happened, and we only left home a couple of hours ago."

"Right? And even though some of it has been crazy and even terrifying, I wouldn't trade any of it for anything," Andi said.

"Neither would I. You're a pretty great road trip companion, Andiman."

"Yay." Andi clapped her hands. "So are you—*and* a really great mom, too."

Chapter 16

After polishing off two plates of truly delicious onion rings and burgers, along with about half the bucket of peanuts, Bex and Andi were eager to get back on the road. But when Bex reached into her brown patchwork suede purse to find her wallet so they could pay the check, she groaned.

"What's wrong?" Andi asked.

"My wallet . . ." Bex said, dumping out the contents of her bag on the table and searching through a mess of keys, sunglasses, lip gloss, receipts, and phone. "I can't find my wallet!"

"Are you sure?" Andi grabbed the purse and checked to make sure the lining was intact, then looked in all the little zippered pockets. But Bex was right: her wallet wasn't there.

"Oh, man." Bex sighed. "That means we have *no* money and it also means we have *no* tickets to get into Mountain Jam!"

Andi couldn't believe it. How could this have happened? "Did you maybe leave it back at the repair shop?"

"I guess it's possible—or maybe it fell out somewhere between there and here." Bex frowned. "I'm really not doing so well with this whole responsible thing, am I?"

"Don't say that!" Andi insisted. "You've been awesome at helping me feel safe, even during some super-scary moments . . . like I was even kind of scared of Jagger and his friends at first, but they wound up totally saving us!" Andi laughed.

"I know—that was pretty funny," Bex said. "I could tell you were worried when they got out of the truck, but Jagger's the best. They were all so nice."

"They were," Andi said, but then thought back to that moment in the truck when Luke chewed on his lower lip. "I'm not so sure about that Luke guy, though. I actually think he was lying about having VIP passes."

That was when something else occurred to Andi. "Oh

my gosh! What if he *does* have VIP passes—what if he has *our* VIP passes?"

"Huh?" Bex screwed up her face.

"What if *Luke* is the one who took your wallet?"

Bex shook her head. "No way. Although I guess it's possible that the wallet fell out in the truck."

"Maybe." Andi shrugged. "But either way, I bet they have it."

"Well, there's only one way to find out," Bex said, grabbing her phone from the table and scrolling through her contacts until she found the number Jagger had programmed in.

"Yeah, but if Luke took it, he'll never tell us," Andi pointed out.

"But Jagger might." Bex tried the number once . . . twice . . . three times but then set her phone down on the table in frustration. "Or not. I can't get any service up here."

"Ssso sorry," the waitress said, slithering back to the table. "The cell service can be ssspotty on the mountain. It's better when you get a bit higher up."

"Oh." Bex sighed.

"Can I get you anything elssse?" Tara asked.

"Not unless you have my wallet," Bex replied. "I can't seem to find it. It's either lost or stolen. So I have no way to pay our check."

"Oh, dear!" the waitress said. "What a messs."

"Is there any way we can give you an IOU and then go try to find it?" Andi asked.

"My bosss would never allow that, I'm afraid. One of you will have to stay here while the other looksss for the wallet."

"But we're on our way to Mountain Jam. We don't want to be late!" Andi said, frowning.

"I'm going to Mountain Jam, too," Tara said, and her watery eyes zeroed in on Bex's ring. "Perhapsss we can make a deal!"

Bex cringed. "Please don't say it has anything to do with taking my firstborn!"

Andi laughed and rolled her eyes.

"No—but that ring!" Tara was practically leaping from

one foot to the other. "That ring, that ring, you can give me that ring! It will look so nice with my fessstival dresss."

"Oh, um . . . you mean I can give it to you as collateral?" Bex proposed. "You can wear it to the festival and then return it when I get my wallet back and come back to pay the bill?"

"Yesss!" The waitress clapped her hands and stretched them toward Bex, eager to get the ring. It was pretty loose when she put it on, given how bony her fingers were, but she still seemed delighted by the deal they'd made.

Bex winked at Andi and smiled, then said to Tara, "Please just be careful with it. It's pretty old, but *very preciousss.*"

"Oh, of courssse!" the waitress quickly agreed, admiring the ring as she spun it around on her finger.

With that, Bex and Andi were free to return to the repair shop, pick up the motorcycle, and head for Mountain Jam—where, hopefully, they would be able to find Jagger *and* Bex's wallet. Unless it turned up somewhere in between.

Chapter 17

Bex and Andi didn't find the wallet lying anywhere on the road between the diner and the repair shop, making Andi even more certain that it was in Jagger's truck—or, more than likely, in Luke's pocket. Bex tried to send a text to Jagger and also to Bowie, letting them know that her wallet was missing, along with the VIP passes to the festival. Alas, the messages weren't going through because of the patchy cell service.

At least Manny had done a great job fixing up the tire. Plus he told Bex not to worry about paying him, let alone giving him some jewelry for collateral. ("Not just because you're a friend, but because you've got no money! Good luck finding that wallet and have a great time at the festival!")

Fortunately, the rest of the drive to the festival grounds was pretty smooth. Better yet, even though Bex and Andi no longer had their tickets to get into the festival itself, they would still be able to check in at the Summit Suites— Mountain Jam's exclusive VIP campsite—since Bowie had reserved that separately for them.

"Oh my gosh!" Andi gasped when they got to the check-in area. "This isn't a campsite—it's a *glampsite*!"

Bex nodded slowly, taking it all in. "It really is. I'd heard about places like this, but I've never gotten this close to any of them before!"

Unlike the crowded, dusty, and sometimes muddy camping areas Bex had described from other festivals, the Summit Suites compound was situated on a lush grassy part of the hillside, with several rows of white tents that sat on wooden platforms, each one with its own parking spot. At first, the bald, heavily tattooed guy at the check-in villa gave Bex a hard time because she didn't have her driver's license. But when she explained that her wallet had been lost or possibly even stolen, and then produced a photocopy of the license, along with a backup picture of it on her phone, he was blown away by her impressive planning skills and directed her to tent number twelve.

"Responsible mom for the *win*!" Bex whispered to Andi, pumping a fist in the air as they headed for their tent.

"Yeah, if only you'd taken a picture of our VIP passes, and stored your credit card information in your phone like I keep telling you to do, and—"

"Okay, okay." Bex rolled her eyes. "Baby steps, right?"

Andi laughed and agreed. "Sure. Baby steps."

After they pulled up to tent number twelve, Bex and Andi jumped off the motorcycle and headed inside to unpack their bags, change into their day-one festival wear, and check out the digs—and they were *not* disappointed. Not only were there two full-sized beds with dark wood frames, crisp white linens, and fresh towels rolled up at the foot of each, but the floors were made from gleaming laminated wood and covered with bright orange-and-navy tribal-print rugs. There was also a lounge area with a couch and mini-fridge, as well as a coffee table and a huge welcome basket full of fresh fruit and other goodies.

"Guess we won't be needing those sleeping bags after all, huh?" Bex smiled and fell back onto one of the beds.

"Maybe we don't even need to find my wallet and go into the festival. I'd be pretty happy hanging out here all weekend."

"Seriously!" Andi agreed, grabbing a bunch of grapes from the fruit basket and dropping onto the comfy orange couch. "Although if the tent where we're sleeping is this amazing, imagine what the VIP tents *inside* the festival would have been like!"

"I assure you, they're even *more* amazing," said someone with a familiar voice.

"Bowie?" Andi leapt up from the couch and raced to hug her father, who was standing at the tent opening, holding a huge potted orchid.

"Hey!" Bowie smiled as he entered the tent and set down the orchid on the coffee table. "What do you think of your accommodations?"

"Incredible!" Andi and Bex replied in unison.

"I'm so glad you found us!" Bex added. "I don't know what to do—my wallet is missing, and our passes to the festival were in it."

"Yeah, I got your text." Bowie sat down on the couch.

"You did?" Bex tilted her head. "I didn't think it went through."

"It did, probably right around the time you pulled up to the festival grounds. There are more cell towers up here," Bowie explained.

"Oh yeah, the cell service has always been better up here—but things have been so crazy I kind of forgot about that." Bex grabbed her phone from her bag and scrolled through it. "That means Jagger should have gotten my text, too . . . but he hasn't responded yet."

"I bet he won't." Andi crossed her arms and sat back down on the couch next to Bowie. "I bet he has the wallet and the VIP passes and is having a *great* time on us."

"Jagger Simon, from high school?" Bowie asked, turning to Bex.

"Uh-huh." Bex recapped everything that had happened on the way up the mountain, from the tire blowout to Jagger's taking them to the repair shop to having to use her ring for collateral at the diner.

"Whoa! I'm glad you guys are okay, and it sounds like Jagger actually helped you out." Bowie turned to look into Andi's eyes. "So what makes you think he has the wallet?"

Andi frowned. "Sure, Jagger seems like a nice guy. But there was something I didn't quite trust about one of his friends. I don't know. Maybe I'm being too suspicious."

"I guess I can understand that," Bowie said. "It's easy to start questioning every little thing after going through the kind of stressful stuff you guys just did. I'm sorry the wallet's missing, and I wish I could get more VIP passes so you could see the Orchid Arena."

"But . . . you can't." Andi sighed. When Bowie had shown up in the tent, a small part of her started channeling Ham again, hoping for the best.

"Total bummer, huh?" Bowie put his hand on top of Andi's. "I tried really hard to snag a couple more after I got the text, but those things are like gold around here. The event organizers are super concerned about keeping the crowds in the VIP areas to a minimum—so they wouldn't budge on giving me two more laminates."

Andi didn't want to get upset, but she could feel her nose starting to tingle like it often did when she was about to cry. "That's okay," she said softly. "Thanks for trying."

"Sure." Bowie gave Andi's hand a pat, then stood up and produced two rectangular cards from the back pocket of his jeans. "I *did* manage to get you a couple of general admission tickets, though."

"Really?" Andi's stomach did a little somersault.

"Yeah, I had to scrounge for them, but it's something, right?"

"Yes! Yes! It's totally something. Thank you so much!" Andi jumped up and gave Bowie a hug.

"Unfortunately, I have some more bad news, though," Bowie said, staring at the floor.

"Uh-oh . . . that doesn't sound good." Bex got up from the bed and walked to the lounge area, where she grabbed Andi's hand and squeezed it tight.

"What is it?" Andi's voice cracked, and she pressed her lips together as she searched Bowie's eyes for a clue.

"Um, well . . . the Renaissance Boys aren't going to be playing tomorrow after all," Bowie said. "Rafe got into a motorcycle accident and is in the hospital."

"Rafe the singer?" Bex asked. "Oh my gosh, that's terrible. Will he be okay?"

"Yeah," Bowie replied. "But not by tomorrow."

Again, Andi's nose started to tingle. She desperately wanted to focus on all the good things she had to look forward to. They still had tickets to the festival . . . *and* they were getting to stay in an amazing tent . . . and at least *they* hadn't been hurt or wound up in the hospital like Rafe. Still, it wasn't exactly what she had been expecting. Of course, Ham had already pointed out that when you expected the best, there was always the chance you'd be disappointed. What else had he said, though? *But I also get to enjoy each moment as it happens.*

Andi decided, right then and there, that that was what she was going to do. No matter how many disappointments came her way on the trip, she was still making the best of it, and she would continue to do that. Yes, she was going to seize the day, embrace and enjoy each moment as it happened—even if those moments didn't include VIP passes or seeing the Renaissance Boys.

Chapter 18

As it turned out, even without VIP access, being at Mountain Jam was better than anything Andi could have expected. From the moment she and Bex stepped off the Summit Suites shuttle, there was so much to see. Sure, it was a music festival, but it was also a festival of other arts. So every aspect of the venue was set up for maximum visual appeal.

Even before she and Bex got to the entrance, Andi could see brightly colored structures everywhere—giant polka-dotted totem poles in every imaginable fluorescent hue, a massive mirror-ball octopus soaring high in the sky, and huge towers of lights near the main stage for the nighttime concerts. Once inside, Andi marveled at all the creative outfits people were wearing—headdresses and belts with dazzling sequins that resembled mermaid scales . . . sheer animal-print scarves fashioned into long robes . . . crocheted skirts and tops and hats . . . and fringe. So much fringe! It was almost like they'd stumbled into a crafting convention, and Andi was already getting all sorts of awesome ideas for things she could make when she got home.

On their way to one of the side stages for the first band's set, Andi and Bex couldn't resist stopping at the petting zoo, where they played with lambs, goats, piglets, and tiny chicks. However, they opted against going into the area containing what amounted to a mini-city made entirely of bounce houses. Andi also declined Bex's invitation to go on any of the carnival rides—especially the Ferris wheel. After all, she still had some pretty bad memories of Jonah's ex-girlfriend, Amber, abandoning her at the top of one after convincing Andi to sneak into the local fairgrounds during that one bizarre sleepover they'd had. That was a long story, and one Andi would rather forget.

Coincidentally, as soon as Amber popped into her head, Andi spotted Jonah, even with the vast sea of people all around—and sure enough, he turned around almost as soon as she set eyes on him. When he saw Andi, he took off his sunglasses and his whole face lit up. He grabbed the hand of a girl who looked like a taller, long-haired version of him, and headed straight for Bex and Andi.

"Hey! You're here!" Jonah dropped the girl's hand and leaned in to give Andi a quick, awkward hug before making introductions. "This is my cousin Mona. Mona, this is my good friend Andi and her mom, Bex."

"*Love* your outfits!" Mona said, pushing her heart-shaped sunglasses onto her head and doing a quick scan of Bex and Andi.

"Thanks—you too," Andi replied, admiring the glittery butterfly wings Mona had attached to the back of her strappy tie-dyed minidress.

"You do look great," Jonah agreed, nodding approvingly at Andi's green embroidered top before reaching out to run a finger over the scarf in her hair. "Cool scarf!"

"Thank you." Andi smiled. Jonah wore plain black cargo shorts and a white graphic skater T-shirt—his typical guy uniform—but Andi said he looked great, too.

"So, Bex," Mona interjected, turning to grab Bex's hand and batting her long, dark, spidery lashes. "Jonah mentioned that you're a makeup artist. Do you maybe want to go check out the beauty stations with me? Jonah absolutely *refuses*, so I am in *desperate* need of some girl time with someone my own age, like, now!"

Bex glanced at Andi, unsure, but Andi insisted that it was fine; she and Jonah could go check out some other stuff for a while, and they could meet up later.

"Are you sure?" Bex looked uncharacteristically nervous about leaving Andi. "I thought we were going to see the Hemlock Brothers' set together."

Andi checked the time on her phone. "They're not going on for another hour, though. Maybe we can meet up then? I'll set a timer on my phone to make sure we get there before they start."

Bex sighed. "Okay, that sounds good. But first . . . *safety* first!"

Bex reached into her leather backpack and produced the smaller red bag. In a flash, she was coating every bit of Andi's exposed skin with a thick layer of sunscreen and handing her the floppy hat, water bottle, and bandanna. "Promise me you'll use these," Bex demanded.

"It's not even that hot or dusty," Andi complained, shoving them all into her strappy white bag.

"It could be later," Bex insisted, sliding a pair of aviator shades over Andi's eyes. "Now, have fun and *please* be careful!"

Andi rolled her eyes. "Trust me?" she asked as Jonah grabbed her elbow and guided her away.

"I trust you!" Bex called out as Andi disappeared into the crowd.

♪ ♫ ♪

Since Jonah had arrived a couple of hours earlier—and had been to Mountain Jam once before—he was already pretty familiar with the setup and had all sorts of suggestions for where they should go and what they should see. After Andi told him everything that had happened to her and Bex on their way up the mountain, including that they had lost their VIP passes, Jonah seemed especially determined to make sure she had fun. First he took her to an incredible art installation with giant balloon animals that were at least thirty feet tall.

"What if it pops?" Andi gasped as she and Jonah posed for a selfie at the base of a metallic-blue balloon dog.

"They're not *really* balloons," Jonah said with a smile. "They're just built to look like they are. I think they're made out of stainless steel or something."

"So cool!" Andi laughed as she and Jonah ran from a pink snake to a purple rabbit and then to a rainbow-hued unicorn.

"It's a balloonicorn!" Jonah laughed and made a goofy face, and Andi did, too, before snapping a photo of their distorted reflections in the metallic unicorn's leg.

"Oh my gosh, I *have* to send that to Buffy and Cyrus!" Andi giggled but then frowned, realizing that anything she sent to her friends from the weekend would make them angry all over again. If only she could have gotten tickets for them!

"Ready for the next stop?" Jonah asked brightly, clearly sensing Andi's somber mood and wanting to cheer her up.

"Oh, um . . . yeah!" Andi said, and she followed Jonah to an area where people were playing all sorts of giant board games, from chess and checkers to Connect 4 and Candy Land.

After playing a few games of checkers, they headed for the area Jonah said Andi would probably love most—the Crafting Coliseum. It was an enormous arena with dozens of booths where people could either buy crafts or make their own. Andi immediately spotted a huge tent with a sign that read DIY FLOWER CROWNS.

"I'll make one for you if you make one for me!" Jonah proposed.

"Okay!" Andi agreed.

After exploring buckets upon buckets of real and artificial flowers, colorful ribbons, organza, and more, Andi and Jonah selected their materials and went to separate tables to privately craft each other's crowns. When they were both satisfied with their work, they reunited and presented the fabulous new floral headpieces they'd created: Jonah made Andi's with big orange and yellow gerbera daisies, and Andi made Jonah's with black and white satin roses. As they placed the crowns on their heads, Andi heard the alarm on her phone going off and checked the screen. "Oh! It's time to go find Bex and Mona."

In spite of the huge crowd already gathered near the stage for the band's set, Andi and Jonah managed to spot Bex and Mona within a few minutes of arriving.

"Aw! Your crowns look so awesome!" Bex smiled. "Did you guys have fun?"

"So much!" Andi said. "And it looks like you did, too. . . . I almost didn't recognize you."

Bex and Mona had both gotten serious glitter make-overs. Bex's lips were covered in blue glitter, while Mona had opted for green, and they both had gold glitter around their eyes and pale pink shimmer on their cheeks. Plus they had sparkly round and star-shaped rhinestones lining the tops of their eyebrows.

"Do you like?" Mona asked, placing one hand on her hip and extending the other arm high in the air.

"Yeah, you both look so shiny!" Jonah smiled.

"Thank you. Shiny is my favorite color," Mona replied with a laugh.

"Hey, is that Bowie?" Jonah asked, taking off his sunglasses and squinting at someone near the stage.

Andi followed Jonah's line of sight and immediately recognized Bowie's mop of dark curls. "Yeah!"

"Bowie!" Bex shouted out, and waved.

Miraculously, he heard his name through the crowd and headed over.

"Hey!" Bowie gave Jonah a high five and then shook Mona's hand after Jonah introduced them.

"How's it going?" Andi asked. "Are you finished with the orchid deliveries? Can you hang out and enjoy the festival now?"

Bowie nodded. "Yup. My work here is done. Although . . . I do have some kind of crazy news."

"What is it?" Bex asked.

"Turns out the Renaissance Boys *might* be back on the schedule—but only if *I* fill in for Rafe."

"*What?* That's *amazing!*" Andi threw her arms around Bowie and hugged him.

"Seriously, man—that's beyond awesome," Jonah agreed.

But Bowie didn't seem nearly as enthusiastic. "Yeah, honestly? I'm not sure I can pull it off."

"Of course you can!" Andi insisted.

"Totally!" Jonah agreed. "You'll completely rock."

"You *have* to do it, Bowie," Bex interjected. "Don't you?"

Bowie grimaced. "I don't know. I've gotten so used to my nice, chill life, working with the plants—and in all honesty, plants make a *much* better audience than people."

"Seriously?" Bex narrowed her eyes, more than a little skeptical.

"Oh, most definitely." Bowie got a blissful look on his face. "They blossom and grow and appreciate me for exactly who I am . . . and they never boo or make me feel like I'm totally bombing."

Andi scowled. "But you won't bomb. You're such a great singer, and you would basically be saving the whole festival. I mean, think about how psyched everyone will be if the Renaissance Boys are back on!"

"But *will* they be psyched when they realize it's me singing and not Rafe?"

"We will!" Bex said, giving Bowie's shoulder a squeeze.

"I dunno, man. I feel like that part of my life is over," Bowie insisted, staring into Andi's eyes. "I really don't miss it—especially now that I have *you* in my life."

Andi searched Bowie's face, certain he wasn't being completely honest. But this time his eye wasn't twitching at all. Was he actually telling the truth? Would he honestly rather work at a nursery and hang out with Andi than headline a huge music festival? In a way, that made her feel nice. But it also seemed like he was giving up on a fun, exciting part of himself.

Andi couldn't help wondering if she was at least partly to blame for that. How could he not be leaping at this chance? How could Andi make him see that it was the opportunity of a lifetime?

Chapter 19

Andi decided that once Bowie watched some of the other bands performing at the festival, he would realize that he *had* to get up and play, too. But unfortunately, the Hemlock Brothers didn't have a particularly great set. First their sound cut out, then the guitar went out of tune, and at one point it was pretty obvious that the singer had forgotten some lyrics. Eventually, the crowd started to dwindle. Even Bex turned to Andi before the band had finished playing and asked if she wanted to go get matching henna tattoos or something.

"Oh, um . . ." Andi thought about the plan she had made to get matching tattoos with Buffy and knew how upset her friend would be if Andi returned from the weekend sporting any sort of henna. "Shouldn't we be trying to track down Jagger and his friends so you can get your wallet back? Did he ever reply to your text?"

Bex pulled the phone out of her leather bag and saw that there *was* a reply from Jagger. "He says he didn't see it, but he'll check the truck when he gets back to their tent tonight and let me know."

"Oh." Andi pouted.

"So? Tattoos?" Bex widened her eyes hopefully.

"I can't. . . . I sort of promised Buffy I'd do that with her, so I'd feel weird doing it with anyone else."

Bex draped an arm around Andi's shoulders. "You're a really good friend."

"Then why don't I feel like one?"

"What would make you feel better?" Bex asked.

"Having Buffy and Cyrus here."

"Okay, but what would make you feel better that we can actually make happen?" Bex tried again.

Andi glanced over at Bowie, who—along with Jonah and Mona—actually seemed to be enjoying the band's performance. "Honestly? I feel like I need to convince Bowie to do the show with the Renaissance Boys."

"Hmmm." Bex nodded. "Then let's convince him!"

"But how?"

"We have to show him what he'll be missing."

Andi looked over at Bowie again. As she watched him put his fingers in his mouth to whistle for the Hemlock Brothers, who were just wrapping up their set, she knew Bex was right. Moments later, Andi and Bex had shared the plan with Jonah and Mona. Together, they would go from one stage to the next, making sure Bowie saw as many bands performing as possible. If that didn't give him the itch to perform himself, nothing would.

It all seemed to be going pretty well at first. The next band they saw was stylistically similar to the Renaissance Boys, and Bowie was definitely getting into their performance along with the rest of the crowd. After each song, the applause got even more enthusiastic, with people screaming out band members' names and "You rock!" and "We love you!" Bowie totally bobbed his head along with the crowd and pumped his fists in the air, whistling and cheering.

"See?" Andi gave Bowie's shoulder a squeeze after the

applause had died down. "People are so into the music here. How can you even *think* about depriving them of that? How sad will they be if they don't get to hear the Renaissance Boys tomorrow?"

"Pretty sad?" Bowie guessed.

"Exactly!" Then Andi came up with a brilliant, if slightly cheesy, argument: "And if you really think about it, depriving all these people of hearing the Renaissance Boys would be as cruel as depriving a plant of sunlight . . . or water . . . or, you know, compost! But if you get up on that stage? They'll be like these thirsty, hungry flowers finally getting to blossom in the presence of your music."

Bowie's eyes grew wide and he nodded slowly. "Whoa. That's pretty deep."

Jonah, who had been standing on the other side of Bowie, chimed in, "It's also pretty true, man. I mean, I'm completely in awe of people who can make music like you do."

"Yeah?" Bowie tilted his head.

"Totally," Jonah said. "I wish I had half the talent that you do."

"Nah." Bowie rolled his eyes and shook his head, the picture of humility. "I bet you have *at least* half my talent—maybe you just haven't discovered it yet."

As Bowie turned his attention back to the band onstage, Andi pulled Jonah aside and whispered urgently, "What are we going to do? I really thought you had him there for a minute."

"And I thought *you* did." Jonah kicked the toe of his black sneaker into the grass.

"I feel like the next performance we see is going to have to really blow him away," Andi said.

"Yeah," Jonah agreed. "We'll just have to hope for the best, I guess."

Sadly, the next performance was a bit of a disappointment—and then, after the band left the stage, one of the Mountain Jam announcers got up and told the crowd that it was time for the Community Open Mic. "If you have something you'd like to share—a song or a poem, art or dance—come on up here and connect with us!"

Andi sighed. How could Bowie possibly get inspired by anyone now? Within minutes, some people near the front of the stage had grabbed instruments and a jam session had taken shape. Andi looked over at Bowie, hoping against hope that he would get up there and start singing. Maybe this was actually the perfect moment for him to get a taste of what it would be like if he decided to perform with the Renaissance Boys!

But then Andi heard someone else singing. She turned her attention to the stage, where an incredibly charismatic guy was belting out what sounded like an original ballad—or at least it wasn't a song Andi had heard before. As his dark curls fell into his eyes and he got more and more into the song, Andi got chills. Not only did he look kind of like Bowie, but he had the most intense, soulful voice. Apparently, Andi wasn't the only one who was blown away; the other people onstage, who had been jamming on bongos and keyboard, bass and guitar, either got quiet or stopped playing altogether so the guy's voice could be the focus. Meanwhile, the crowd grew larger and larger as passersby heard this incredible singer and stopped to listen.

By the time the guy wrapped up his performance, at least a hundred people were crowded around, all cheering like crazy—including Andi, Bex, and Bowie. The singer must have been in a serious zone while he was up there, because he suddenly looked out at the crowd as if he were waking up from a dream and had no idea how he'd gotten there. The other musicians on the stage embraced him or shook his hand, and then he jumped down into the crowd, where throngs of people began asking him if he had any recordings they could buy or if they could at least get his autograph.

"Wow," Bex gushed, turning to look at Andi and the others. "That was incredible."

"It really was," Andi agreed, glancing over at Bowie. "Do you have any idea who that was?"

"Not a clue," Bowie replied in a hushed tone. Andi studied Bowie's face. At first she thought his eyes were filling up with tears, and she worried that he might be bummed about this super-talented complete unknown getting so much love from the crowd, not to mention from Bex and Andi. But then she realized his eyes weren't teary; they looked like a fire had been lit behind them.

"So what are you thinking?" Andi said to Bowie.

"I'm thinking"—Bowie paused and took a deep breath—"that I really should have gotten up on that stage before *that guy* did."

Andi gasped. Had the plan worked? Had Bowie been inspired to do a bit of singing himself?

"But since I didn't," Bowie continued, "I guess I'm going to have to get up on the *main* stage . . . tomorrow night . . . with the Renaissance Boys!"

"Really?" Andi bounced up and down, her heart racing. "You're actually going to do it?"

"Yep." Bowie smiled as Andi, Bex, Jonah, and Mona engulfed him in a massive group hug. "I'm actually going to do it."

Chapter 20

As soon as Bowie gave the Renaissance Boys the good news about his decision to perform with them, Mountain Jam got better and better—thanks in large part to the fact that the band gave Bowie *eight* VIP passes.

"What am I gonna do with the rest of these passes?" Bowie wondered after handing the first four to Andi, Bex, Jonah, and Mona. "I guess I could wander around the festival and make a few random people's days?"

"Actually . . ." Andi had a much better idea. "Maybe Pops and CeCe could use them—and if it's not too much to ask, could I see if they might be able to bring Buffy and Cyrus, too?"

"Andi." Bex's tone was sharp as she narrowed her eyes. "You seriously think Pops and CeCe are going to want to drive up *here*, after everything CeCe said—after the way she made it sound like the world's most dangerous road trip and did everything she could think of to stop us from going?"

"Ham definitely will," Bowie interjected. "He already asked if I could get tickets for him and CeCe, but I couldn't hook him up as a vendor. Now I totally can!" Bowie gave Bex a sly grin and winked before lowering his voice and adding, "I think your dad wants to relive his youth with your mom."

"Ew." Bex grimaced.

"Bowie's right," Andi said. "Pops told me that he and CeCe had plenty of adventures of their own back in the day, including going to music festivals and camping. I think coming here this weekend could be really great for them! Even if they can't get here until tomorrow, they'll still be able to hang out for a while and see the Renaissance Boys, right?"

"Totally." Bowie nodded.

"All right." Bex sighed. "I guess you can at least call them and see what they say."

"Yay!" Andi pulled her phone out of the back pocket of

her white jeans. As soon as Ham answered, she gave him the full rundown at lightning speed: "Bowie's going to fill in for the singer of the Renaissance Boys because he's in the hospital, and so he got a whole bunch of VIP passes for all of us, meaning you can bring CeCe to Mountain Jam after all—if you want to, that is. But if you think you can make it—even if it's not until tomorrow—would you maybe be willing to bring Cyrus and Buffy with you, too?"

Ham chuckled into the phone and Andi could picture his blue eyes sparkling as he processed everything she had told him. "That's fantastic—except the part about the hospital. But good for Bowie! I'll make sure we get up there, one way or another, and I'd be happy to drive Buffy and Cyrus."

"Oh, Pops! Thank you so much! I'll call Buffy and Cyrus now. Just let me know how soon you can get up here. Can't wait to see you!"

Andi's hands were trembling as she tried to decide who to call next. She was a little worried that Buffy might not pick up—but she also worried that Buffy would be upset if Andi called Cyrus first.

"Hey," Buffy said tersely after waiting three rings to answer. "How's Mountain Jam?"

Andi squeezed her eyes shut and took a deep breath. "It's been fun, but it would be so much more fun if you were here."

"Well, we know that's not gonna happen."

"Actually, it could! Bowie got a bunch of VIP passes because he's going to be filling in for the singer of the Renaissance Boys. So Pops and CeCe are going to drive up, and Pops said he would bring you and Cyrus with them—I mean . . . if you want to. Please say you want to!"

There was a painfully long pause, but at last Buffy replied, "Okay."

"Okay?" Andi frowned. "That's it?"

"I mean, okay . . . see you soon, I guess? And thanks?"

"You're welcome," Andi said. "Um. See you soon!"

As much of a bummer as the call with Buffy had been, the one with Cyrus was way better. Andi could practically see him bouncing off the walls of his bedroom when she gave him the news. He hung up almost as quickly as

Buffy had—but only because, as he told Andi, he wanted to start figuring out what to pack.

Having agonized over her own wardrobe, Andi completely understood that.

Chapter 21

Once plans with Pops and CeCe were confirmed—they would arrive bright and early the next morning and bring Buffy and Cyrus with them—Andi was ready to celebrate. And what better place to do that than in the VIP area—also known as the Orchid Arena? The big white tents were located right next to the main stage, allowing for the best possible view of all the biggest acts.

After flashing their laminates, Andi and the rest of the group were shuttled past red velvet ropes and through brightly colored gauze drapes. Inside the tents were enough white leather massage chairs and couches for each and every VIP guest, and Bowie's orchids looked gorgeous sitting on heavy black marble tables. The only thing missing was Bowie, who was rehearsing with the band in anticipation of the next night's performance.

"Check it out!" Jonah said, making a beeline for a table with a chocolate fountain towering at least four feet high, surrounded by bowls of fresh fruit, fluffy white marshmallows, puff pastries, fancy cookies, and more.

Bex grabbed a skewer and speared a piece of pineapple, then held it under the cascading chocolate. Meanwhile, Mona opted for a marshmallow, and Andi and Jonah both selected rolled wafer cookies.

"Oh my gosh . . . that might just be the most delicious chocolate I've ever tasted!" Mona smiled, and they all laughed at how her glittery green lips were smeared with chocolate and marshmallow.

"Seriously!" Jonah agreed. "And look over there."

On the other side of the tent was an entire section devoted to carnival food, including a red-and-white popcorn machine, a bright pink cotton candy stand, funnel cakes, hot dogs, and every deep-fried food known to man. Then, in the next tent over, there was a DJ commanding an enormous dance floor filled with people.

"Incredible." Andi's skin was tingling as she took it all in.

"It really is—thank you so much for hooking us up with passes to get into this place," Jonah said, smiling at Andi. "I thought last year was fun, but this is beyond anything I could have imagined."

"Me too." Andi smiled back. "But don't thank me, thank Bowie."

"Well, if it weren't for you, I wouldn't know Bowie . . . right?"

"I guess." Andi grinned, but then her expression clouded over when she saw a familiar face. It was Luke, with Jagger and Zane right behind him.

Andi turned to Bex and grabbed her by the arm. "Look who it is," she whispered.

Bex followed the direction of Andi's eyes and waved when she saw Jagger and the others. "Jagger! Over here!"

"Hey!" Jagger grinned and hugged Bex. "How's it going? How awesome is this setup?"

"So awesome!" Bex agreed.

"I guess you found your wallet, then?" Jagger asked, motioning to the rainbow-hued VIP laminate sitting on top of Bex's silver-and-turquoise neckpiece.

"Oh, um . . . no," Bex said. "But you remember Bowie from high school?"

"Of course." Jagger raised his dark eyebrows and gave Bex a light punch on her bare upper arm. "You guys were quite the item."

"Yeah, well, he's going to be filling in for the Renaissance Boys' singer tomorrow, so he managed to get more VIP passes for us."

"That rules!" Jagger grinned.

"Yeah, it does," Andi interjected, glancing over at Luke. "But it's been kind of stressful, wondering where the wallet went."

"That's such a bummer," Luke replied, "but hopefully you've still been able to have a good time so far?"

Once again, Luke was chewing on his lower lip and Andi couldn't shake the feeling that he was hiding something. Maybe he hadn't taken the wallet, but something was up with the guy. If only Andi could figure out what it was.

Chapter 22

  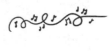

"Can you excuse us for a minute?" Bex asked Jagger and his friends with a forced smile, grabbing Andi by the elbow and guiding her over to the other side of the chocolate fountain.

"Andi, I know you think Luke took the wallet, but you have no way of proving that," Bex whispered impatiently. "Can you please just let it go, at least until they get a chance to search their truck for it?"

Andi stared at the dark wood floor and crossed her arms. "I guess—but don't you think there's something off about that guy? I think he has a dark side."

Bex laughed. "Maybe Darth Vader finally got to him?"

Andi narrowed her eyes, not getting it at first.

"Luke, I am your father!" Bex said in her deepest, most ominous voice.

"Oh. Ha." Andi forced a laugh.

"Come on," Bex groaned. "Lighten up and let it go . . . at least for now. We got new VIP passes, so let's enjoy them!"

Andi thought about it for a second and knew Bex was right. So she agreed to stop worrying—for now anyway— and they joined the others.

"Everything okay?" Jagger asked.

"Everything's great!" Bex flashed a smile.

"Cool—then you guys should come check out the VR tent!" Jagger proposed, looking directly at Mona. He hadn't stopped staring at her since they were introduced, and Mona had been staring right back at him.

"What's VR?" Mona asked.

"Virtual reality," Jonah replied with a scowl.

Andi gave him a sympathetic frown. She knew he was thinking back to that fall he took at the arcade.

"Cool! Let's do it!" Mona said, bouncing on her heels so her glittery butterfly wings fluttered.

"Actually . . ." Jonah hesitated.

"Why don't you guys go ahead?" Andi interrupted,

sensing that Jonah didn't want to get into the details. "Jonah and I . . . um . . . still have a bunch of other stuff we want to see outside. Right?"

Andi turned to Jonah, who nodded gratefully.

"But what about all the stuff to see in here?" Bex widened her eyes at Andi. "We're VIPs now! At least come check out the massage chairs with me!"

Andi laughed and shook her head. "Maybe a little later?"

Bex glanced from Andi to Jonah and knew she wasn't going to win this one. "Okay . . . but first . . ."

"No!" Andi squealed. "No more safety first!"

"Just a little more sunscreen," Bex pressed, already squeezing some from the tube onto her finger and delicately dabbing it on Andi's nose and cheeks.

"Okay, I'm good!" Andi insisted, swatting Bex away. "Can we please go now?"

"Yes, you can go," Bex finally agreed. "But keep your phone close, and text me in an hour to let me know you're . . . *safe*."

"Thanks for doing that," Jonah said with a sheepish smile after he and Andi had exited the Orchid Arena.

"Sure—that's what friends are for."

"Where should we go next?" Jonah wondered, pulling a festival map from his pocket and holding it out so Andi could scan it with him. They agreed to go check out the carnival area.

"But I'm *not* going on the Ferris wheel," Andi warned Jonah.

"Oh, man, I forgot about that." He grimaced.

He obviously knew Andi was referring to the sleepover disaster with Amber. So when they arrived at the carnival area, Jonah took Andi as far away from the Ferris wheel as they could get—which meant they went directly to the Skyscraper Slide.

Andi could feel her palms sweating when Jonah proposed that they go on it. She looked up at the slide, towering high above them, and swallowed hard.

"It's way too steep," Andi said, her lips trembling. "But you can go without me if you want."

Andi could see from the look on Jonah's face that he

was beyond disappointed. Andi was kind of disappointed in herself, too. She had already done so many things to prove how adventurous and unpredictable she could be— so why was she playing it safe with the slide? She glanced up again and her stomach dropped.

"I'm sorry," Andi said with a frown. "You should really go without me."

"You sure?" Jonah pouted, blinking his eyes in that pleading puppy-dog way.

Andi looked up one last time and nodded. So Jonah handed his flower crown to Andi to hold—"I don't want to lose it on the way down," he explained—and joined the line of brave souls waiting to ascend the stairs. Meanwhile, Andi headed to the waiting area, where people were screaming and laughing and watching everyone plummet to the bottom. When it was finally Jonah's turn, Andi got her phone out and took a slo-mo video of him making his descent, whooping and hollering the entire way down.

"Dude! That was out of control!" Jonah enthused when he had exited the ride and found Andi.

"You know what was really out of control?" Andi laughed.

"What?"

"How loud you screamed!" Andi handed her phone to Jonah so he could play back the video.

"I'm not screaming!" Jonah scoffed after watching the video. "That's a victory yell."

"Uh-huh." Andi laughed again.

"Seriously, you have no clue what you're missing."

"And I would rather remain clueless," Andi replied as she noticed the most bizarre thing heading toward her and Jonah. "What *is* that?"

Jonah turned to look, and as it got closer, they both scrunched up their faces in disbelief.

"I think it's a giant walking pizza?" Jonah said.

"I think you're right!"

"Who wants pizza?" came a male voice from somewhere deep within the pizza costume, which was prancing through the crowd, stopping to let various people take selfies.

"Look at his back!" Andi pointed to a poster stuck to the costume. "It says, 'Follow me to the pizza-eating contest'!"

"Dude." Jonah gasped. "Now's my chance!"

With a mischievous smile, Andi said, "I'll do it if you do."

"Are you kidding me?" Jonah shook his head. "There's no way you're going to enter."

"Oh, yes, there is," Andi insisted. "It's in my blood—Bex entered one year and took third place."

Jonah's eyes grew wide. "Well, okay then. I guess we'd better go check it out."

"I guess we'd better!"

So Jonah and Andi joined the crowd of people who were following the giant pizza. Andi wasn't going to back down this time. She would prove to Jonah—and more important, to herself—that she could be as daring and adventurous as he was. So long as it didn't involve slides as tall as skyscrapers.

Chapter 23

After winding through crowds of people, the giant pizza finally arrived at the entrance to an outdoor amphitheater with a digital billboard that read EXTREME EATING ARENA, along with a scrolling list of the schedule of food-eating events, which had kicked off earlier in the day with pancakes. That had been followed by hot dogs, hamburgers, buffalo wings, and pies. Pizza was up next, and later they would have a rib-eating contest and a giant turkey leg–eating contest.

"Excuse me! Comin' through!" said someone behind Andi and Jonah, and they turned to see half a dozen people in red pizza delivery uniforms, each one wheeling a metal utility cart holding what must have been at least fifty pizzas.

Andi looked over at Jonah, who was bouncing from foot to foot as though he couldn't wait to get inside.

"Is your mouth watering as much as mine is?" Andi asked.

"Uh-huh!" Jonah motioned for Andi to follow him along the sloping concrete path right behind the pizza delivery people, who were making their way toward the stage at the bottom of the amphitheater. "I hope it's not too late to enter!"

"Oh, no—I didn't even think about that." Andi glanced at the stage, where people in bright yellow EVENT STAFF shirts were cleaning off a table covered in what appeared to be blueberry pie. Off to one side, contestants wearing formerly white bibs—also covered in pie, Andi assumed—were walking over to a smaller table covered in red, white, and blue ribbons with a sign that read WINNERS' CIRCLE. Next to that table was another one labeled SIGN-UP CENTRAL.

"There!" Jonah yelled. "That's where we enter!"

Andi continued to follow Jonah, but when they got to the end of the line of people waiting to add their names to the sign-up sheet, they saw a guy in one of the pie-covered bibs running toward them. He had short, spiky brown hair and his round face was flushed and sweaty—and also covered in pie.

"Look out!" the guy yelled, shoving past the line of people waiting to enter the pizza-eating contest.

Andi and Jonah watched in horror as he stumbled by them and finally arrived at his destination. Like a man reuniting with his long-lost love, the guy wrapped his arms around the top edge of the black garbage bin and proceeded to make awful retching noises into it.

Andi cringed as she looked over at Jonah, whose face had gone pale. "Are you okay?" she asked.

"No!" Jonah groaned, slapping a hand over his mouth. "If we don't get out of here soon, I think I'm going to be sick, too."

Andi looked over at the stage again, where the pizzas were being set up on the long competition table, and then took a few steps closer to the sign-up table. There were only a few more people in front of them, and Andi *really* wanted to enter. But when she turned to look at Jonah again, she noticed he was breaking out in a cold sweat and turning a little green.

"So maybe we should skip the pizza?" she asked with a frown. Who knew Jonah got queasy so easily?

Jonah nodded fervently. "Yes, please!" He spun around and headed toward the ramp leading out of the arena so quickly that Andi had to jog to keep up.

When they were safely outside, Jonah turned to Andi, and she was relieved to see that he didn't look nearly as green.

"Feeling better?" she asked.

"Ugh." He exhaled loudly. "I'm really sorry—I knew people sometimes got upset stomachs at these things, but I've never seen it happen up close. If we hadn't left, I would one hundred percent have thrown up."

"I was feeling pretty queasy on the ride up the mountain earlier, so I totally get it."

"Thanks for understanding—and thanks for getting out of there with me," Jonah said with a frown. "I don't know what I would have done if I was with any of my other friends. They're all so crazy, they probably would have forced me to go through with it."

"Uh-huh." Andi knew she had probably made the right call by leaving the pizza-eating contest, but she was still determined to show Jonah that he was wrong about her. She could take risks! She could be wild and crazy! And in fact, now that she had seen his slightly less courageous side, she felt as though it was time to show *her* more courageous side to him . . . and to herself.

"You know what?" Andi suddenly said, pushing past Jonah and through the crowd.

"What?" Jonah asked, chasing after her.

"I'm going on the Skyscraper Slide!" Andi yelled back.

"*Huh?*" Jonah caught up and grabbed Andi's arm, stopping her. "You don't have to do that!"

"I know I don't *have* to," Andi replied. "But I want to."

When they made it to the slide, however, Andi's heart sank as she counted the flights of stairs to the top.

One step at a time, she told herself. *You can do this.*

With each step she took, her legs became shakier and her stomach filled with more butterflies. But by the time she arrived at the platform, she knew there was no turning back. So she took a deep breath, closed her eyes, and— yes—screamed the entire way down. But when she finally landed at the bottom and stopped screaming, a giant smile spread across her face. Jonah had been right—it really was out of control, but in the best possible way!

"What a rush!" Andi squealed when Jonah got to the bottom. "Want to go again?"

Jonah laughed. "Seriously?"

"Seriously!" Andi insisted, already making her way back to the line.

And this time her legs felt strong and her fear was completely gone.

Chapter 24

When Andi woke up on Sunday morning, she was shivering—partly because it was a lot colder than she had expected it to be, partly because she was so excited that Buffy and Cyrus would be arriving soon with Ham and CeCe, and partly because of how much fun she'd already had at Mountain Jam. The highlight so far had definitely been conquering the Skyscraper Slide; she and Jonah must have gone down that thing almost a dozen times, and each time had been better than the last!

After that, Andi and Jonah had reunited with Bex and Mona in the VIP tent, where they were able to watch all the incredible nighttime performances on the main stage. The bands had been great, but Andi was sure nothing would compare to seeing Bowie play with the Renaissance Boys—yet another thought that gave her chills. They also danced in the DJ area and filled up on way too much carnival food, and Jonah even conquered his fears and played a few games with Andi in the virtual reality tent before wrapping up the evening with an extended stretch—literally—in the massage chairs. The first day and night of Mountain Jam had been epic, to say the least.

"Good morning!" Bex smiled and rolled onto her side. "How'd you sleep?"

"*Really* well." Andi sat up and hugged her knees to her chest. "These beds are *so* comfortable."

"They really are," Bex agreed. "Beats the heck out of our sleeper sofa!"

"I bet." Andi grinned and pulled the covers around her. "But isn't it kind of cold in here?"

"Yeah, kind of." Bex hopped out of her bed and threw a hoodie on over her old gray concert tee and sweatpants, then went to check out the little air-conditioning unit for their tent. "I never thought we'd need to use the heat setting on this thing up here, but hey—at least there is one!"

Andi sighed happily as the tent started to warm up. She got out of bed and put a sweatshirt on over her pink thermal jammies. Then she headed for the couch, where Bex was eating a banana from the fruit basket.

"How soon do you think Pops and CeCe will get here?" Andi wondered.

Bex looked down at her phone. "I'd say by ten?"

"I can't wait!" Andi smiled. "How awesome is it that Bowie was able to get so many VIP passes—*and* that he's going to be playing with the Renaissance Boys tonight?"

"So awesome. Incredible, even." Bex took a deep breath. "Truly incredible—and all thanks to you."

Andi crinkled her nose. "Me?"

"Shyeah!" Bex said. "I mean, if you hadn't come up with that plan to drag him to all those performances—*especially* that open mic—he might never have realized what he'd be missing."

"But that was *your* plan."

"Well, it was *our* plan . . . and you and Jonah really made it happen."

Andi thought about it for a moment. "Yeah, I guess so. Maybe . . ."

Bex shivered and walked over to the tent opening,

taking a quick peek at the sky. "I can't believe how cold it is today! It's even cloudy—I hope it doesn't rain."

Andi frowned. "Do you think it will?"

"I hope not. But at least I brought those rain ponchos, and we may need to rethink today's outfits a bit and dress in layers. Hopefully the clouds will burn off, but you never know up here in the mountains."

Fortunately, the gauzy yellow tunic Andi had been planning to wear looked super cute over the jeans she'd worn on the ride up to the festival the day before—and Bex still looked like a bohemian goddess, even with leggings under her tie-dyed skirt and a long-sleeved white thermal under her leather vest.

"I'll just pack the tank top in my backpack and change out of the thermal if it warms up later," Bex noted.

Once all their primping was out of the way, Bex and Andi were ready to board the shuttle and head for the Orchid Arena to meet up with the others. When they arrived in the main tent, Andi spotted Buffy and Cyrus immediately—mostly because Cyrus was laughing hysterically and screaming "That tickles!" while trying out a massage chair. Meanwhile, Buffy was standing over him and trying to shush him.

Andi ran over and gave Buffy a huge hug from behind, then pulled Cyrus out of the chair and hugged him, too.

"Thank you!" Buffy sighed and tilted her head at Cyrus. "All that laughter was getting embarrassing."

"Maybe for *you*, but my parents say it's extremely important to laugh loud and laugh often," Cyrus replied, holding up an index finger. Then, quickly switching topics, he scanned Andi from head to toe. "So you look faaabulous!"

"Thanks," Andi replied. "You both look fabulous, too!"

Buffy really did look great. Her dark curls were big and glossy, falling just below her shoulders, and she had on a flowery boho-chic tank beneath a brown suede jacket, along with matching suede lace-up boots and dark skinny jeans. For accessories, she wore a simple leather choker and a few silver bracelets, plus the friendship bracelet she'd made at the sleepover with Andi a few weeks earlier.

Cyrus was decked out in what Andi had come to realize was standard music festival wear for a lot of guys—a

Hawaiian shirt (Cyrus's was dark red with pink flowers), along with black jeans and red sneakers.

"How was the drive up?" Andi added. "Where are Pops and CeCe?"

"Oh, they're already in the disco tent!" Cyrus said. "Those two know how to pa-ar-tay!"

Andi giggled and turned toward the tent with the DJ, only to see Jagger, Luke, and Zane approaching.

"Oh my gosh!" Andi spun back around and grabbed her friends' hands. "I have so much to tell you about yesterday—but the most important thing right now? See those three guys walking this way? I think the one with the blond hair may have stolen Bex's wallet, but he won't admit it!"

Cyrus craned his neck to look over Andi's shoulder and she gave his arm a light smack. "Don't look at them!"

"But you said, 'See those three guys,'" Cyrus loud-whispered. "I'm just following directions!"

Andi sighed. "Okay, okay. My point is . . . we *have* to figure out if they're lying or not." Andi stared into Cyrus's dark eyes and gave him and Buffy a quick recap of what had happened on the way up the mountain—the flat tire, Jagger picking them up in his truck because he and Bex went to high school together, Luke chewing on his lower lip and saying they had VIP passes, and then the wallet going missing. "How are your lie-detector skills this morning?"

"My lie-detector skills are always *en fuego*," Cyrus said, slowly nodding and winking. "That means 'on fire' in Spanish, of course."

"Of course," Andi replied impatiently. "Then get ready to bring the heat—they're here."

Jagger was the first to tap Andi on the shoulder. "Hey, Andi! How's it going?"

"Good!" Andi pasted on a smile and turned around. "How are you guys?"

"Awesome!" they all replied at the same time.

"Where's Bex?" Jagger asked, running a hand over his slicked-back hair. He was wearing the exact same thing he'd had on the day before—white T-shirt, black leather jacket, jeans—and Zane and Luke also appeared to be wearing their same jeans, flannels, and T-shirts.

"Oh, um, I'm not sure," Andi replied. "I think she went to find our . . . I mean *her* parents—Pops and CeCe to me."

Jagger chuckled. "Wow—hanging with the 'rents at Mountain Jam. Cool!"

Eager to get to the lie detecting, Andi turned to Buffy and Cyrus and introduced them to Jagger, Luke, and Zane.

"Great to meet you cats," Cyrus said, attempting some weird kind of guy handshake with each of them that eventually ended in everyone awkwardly crossing their arms.

Andi turned to glare at Cyrus and gave him a sly but suggestive few taps on the arm.

"Oh!" Cyrus bounced on his feet a few times. "There's, um, so much I'd like to know about you guys. Andi mentioned that you *really* helped her and Bex out yesterday after they got a flat tire. True or false?"

Jagger's chiseled features broke into an amused smile. "Uhhh . . . true?"

"And, Luke," Cyrus continued. "Such an interesting name! Are you the child of *Star Wars* fans . . . or, perhaps, did they give you that name because of the late-seventies soap opera power couple Luke and Laura?"

Luke's blue eyes widened. He leaned in close to Cyrus and whispered, "Dude. I usually tell people it's because of *Star Wars*, but my mom was *obsessed* with *General Hospital*. I can't believe you know about that show!"

Cyrus smiled and gave Luke a pat on the shoulder. "Your secret's safe with me, buddy," he whispered back.

After Cyrus had run the guys through half a dozen more questions, Jagger finally cut him off. "Hey, this has been fun, but we really need to get over to the Sierra Stage or we'll miss the Cavemen—they go on at eleven."

"Right on, my man," Cyrus said. "Love the Cavemen! See you there, maybe!"

"Cool!" Jagger and his friends gave little waves and walked away.

"So? What do you think?" Andi asked Cyrus as soon as they were out of earshot.

Cyrus shook his head and stared at the laminated wood floor. "I'm sorry, Andi, but those are three of the most honest people I've ever met in my life—*especially*

Luke. I don't think that dude would be capable of stealing *anything*, let alone lying about it."

"Darn it," Andi muttered. "But you didn't even ask him about the wallet."

"I know. But I feel quite confident in my interrogation methods. There must be some other explanation for the missing wallet," Cyrus insisted. "Any other theories?"

Before Andi could reply, Buffy turned to Cyrus. "I don't have any theories about the wallet, but I *do* have a theory about your breath."

Cyrus immediately clapped a hand over his mouth. "Oh, no! Is it bad?"

Buffy grimaced and nodded apologetically. "Might be time for a breath mint?"

The moment Buffy said the words "breath mint," Andi's memory was jogged. She, too, clapped a hand over her mouth, and then she reached into her backpack. After rifling around for a few minutes, her fingers touched the edge of Bex's wallet, and she felt light-headed—almost as if she was going to pass out. She grabbed Buffy by the arm to steady herself.

"What is it?" Buffy asked, noticing the pained expression on Andi's face.

Andi cringed as she pulled Bex's wallet from her backpack and flipped it open, allowing the two original VIP passes to dangle down from their purple lanyards. "Mystery solved."

"But . . . how is that possible?" Cyrus asked.

"When Jagger gave us a ride to the repair shop, my stomach was growling like crazy," Andi explained, replaying the events in her mind. "So Bex gave me her wallet because it had some old mints stuck to the bottom of it!"

"Oh my gosh . . ." Buffy gasped.

"I totally forgot that I put the wallet in my backpack instead of giving it back to her." Andi frowned. "I think I was just in a hurry to get out of the truck. All this time I thought Luke was guilty, when, in reality, I'm the guilty one."

Andi felt as though she might cry.

"It's okay," Cyrus said softly. "These things happen."

"But why did it have to happen to me . . . this weekend?" Andi said.

"You do seem to be messing up quite a bit lately," Buffy noted coolly, crossing her arms.

Ouch. Andi had expected both of her friends to help her feel better. But she realized she still might need to work on making *Buffy* feel better first.

Chapter 25

Glossing over Buffy's comment for the moment, Andi proposed that they go find Bex so she could give her back the wallet and also say hi to CeCe and Ham. Sure enough, they were all in the DJ area, and CeCe was throwing down some impressive moves on the dance floor—moves Andi and Bex had only recently realized CeCe had when she let them tag along to one of her dance classes. CeCe and Ham had dressed for the occasion: CeCe wore an olive-green maxi dress with white floral embroidery, and Ham was in a blue-and-gray bowling shirt and jeans.

Thankfully, Bex was completely understanding about the whole wallet situation, and noted that it seemed way more like something *she* would have done.

"Not true," Andi insisted. "You've been so on top of everything this weekend—making sure I was okay when

I got queasy *and* after we got the flat tire . . . planning ahead with the driver's license thing, which meant we could still get into our Summit Suite . . . going way overboard with making me wear sunscreen and layers and—"

"Okay, okay!" Bex laughed. "When you put it that way, I guess I deserve the Mother of the Year Award!"

"You kind of do," Andi agreed. "Not only are you great at taking care of me, but you make my whole life more fun and exciting, too."

"So you're really not bored anymore?" Bex asked.

"No way!"

"Awww." Bex sighed and ran a finger over the little feathers in Andi's dream catcher headband.

"But since you're Mother of the Year," Andi added, pulling Bex to the side, "do you maybe have any motherly advice about how I can finally get Buffy to forgive me? She still seems pretty annoyed that I forgot about our Mountain Jam plans and then lied about it."

"Seriously?" Bex scowled. "That's kind of crazy,

considering how much you've already done to make it up to her. But maybe it's just going to take her a little more time to get over it."

"Maybe . . ."

"A little time and *a lot more Mountain Jam!*" Bex added, clapping her hands and bouncing up and down in her strappy gladiator sandals.

Andi figured Bex was probably right. If she was going to get Buffy to forgive her completely, she would have to make sure Buffy had the absolute best time ever at the festival. And what better way to do that than by taking her around to at least some of the things that had made the previous day so fun for Andi?

Unfortunately, no matter how excited Cyrus got when they visited each new place—from the giant balloon animal area to the Crafting Coliseum—Buffy didn't seem to be feeling it. Sure, she cracked a smile once or twice, but Andi soon began to wonder if there was something else going on with her—something that had nothing to do with Andi's forgetting their original plans.

"Hey!" Andi said, spotting a tent draped in red-and-gold material, with a sign on the front that read TARA'S TATTOOS.

"Oh!" Buffy saw the tent, too, and her whole face lit up.

But before they could take another step toward it, someone came up behind Andi and covered her eyes. "Guess who!"

"Jonah!" Andi laughed, pulling his hands from her eyes and turning around.

"How's it going, guys?" Jonah asked, giving Buffy a wave and high-fiving Cyrus.

"We are *rocking* this jam," Cyrus replied, snapping and shooting a finger gun at Jonah.

"Where's Mona?" Andi asked.

Jonah rolled his eyes and sighed. "At that makeup place again. Honestly, I think she would take a *bath* in glitter if she could."

"She actually can," Cyrus noted in his usual matter-of-fact way.

"Huh?" Andi said. Andi, Buffy, and Jonah all stared at Cyrus in disbelief.

"Oh, yeah." Cyrus shrugged. "It's a whole thing with the kids these days—just don't ask me how I know."

Andi laughed. "We *definitely* won't."

"So what are you up to now?" Jonah asked.

Andi locked eyes with Buffy. "I think we might want to get . . . henna tattoos?"

Buffy blinked a few times and nodded, allowing a tiny hint of a smile to cross her full glossy lips. "Yeah. That would be fun."

"*All* of you?" Jonah asked, shooting a sideways glance at Cyrus.

"Um, that would be a no," Cyrus said. "Tattoos are forbidden by my religion. If I got one, I couldn't be buried in a Jewish cemetery."

Buffy gave Cyrus a light smack on his arm. "They're not *permanent* tattoos, crazy."

"Pssshhh, I know! But why start down that rabbit hole? It could be a gateway to some *serious* ink, and then— BOOM—suddenly I'm erased from the Goodman family cemetery plot . . . *forever*."

"Well, speaking of cemeteries," Jonah said, "I was about to go check out Tombstone Playground's set on the Rockslide Stage. Do you guys want to join?"

"Sure!" Cyrus agreed immediately.

Buffy and Andi locked eyes again, and Buffy shook her head.

"I think Buffy and I are going to stick with the tattoo plan, if that's okay," Andi said. "Maybe we could meet up with you guys after?"

"Totally." Jonah turned to Cyrus. "Ready?"

"Hello? I was *born* ready," Cyrus replied.

As soon as Andi and Buffy went inside the tattoo tent, which smelled of sandalwood incense and was adorned with cushions, rugs, candles, and lamps, Andi heard a familiar voice: "Oh, it looks sssooo preciousss."

Andi squinted at the woman sitting behind an ornately carved wood table as the girls who had just been tattooed handed her some money and slipped out of the tent.

Oh my gosh! Andi looked more closely at the woman behind the table. It was Tara, the waitress from the diner!

Although she had changed out of her little pink uniform and into a colorful bohemian dress and scarf, Andi recognized the voice and those sunken blue eyes right away. But the turquoise ring on her finger sealed the deal. It was definitely her.

"It'sss you, it'sss you!" Tara said, recognizing Andi, too. "You were at the diner yesterday! I have your ring!"

"Well, you have my *mom's* ring," Andi corrected her.

"Please, sssit down!" Tara motioned to two big velvet poufs on the other side of her table.

Buffy shot Andi a look of mild terror but went ahead and sat down next to Andi while Tara clapped her bony hands and said, "You're here for tattoos?"

"Yes," Andi confirmed, putting a hand gently on Buffy's shoulder to reassure her that she was in a safe place. "Matching ones."

"Lovely, lovely," Tara replied, pulling out a binder containing page after page of ornate design options, which Buffy and Andi proceeded to flip through while Tara continued to talk. "I mussst tell you, this ring has brought me so much luck this weekend! My customers have been thrilled with their tattoos. I'm convinced this ring has been helping my technique."

Andi looked up and smiled. "I can understand that."

"Yesss?" Tara asked.

"Sure. I totally feel like certain things I wear make me more creative."

"Exactly!" Tara smiled. "Ssso have you decided on a design?"

Andi looked over at Buffy, who had stopped on a page featuring a beautiful image with all sorts of intertwining leaves and vines. "I think this one?" Buffy turned to look at Andi.

"That's beautiful," Andi agreed, then glanced at Tara. "Does it have any particular meaning?"

"Oh, yesss." Tara nodded solemnly. "Vines and leaves represent longevity, devotion, perseverance—for you, perhaps this would be an expression of your long-lasssting friendship?"

Andi's eyes welled up with tears, and she noticed that Buffy's were doing the same. "That's perfect," Andi said. "Isn't it?"

Buffy took a deep breath. "Yeah. I think so?"

With that, Tara proceeded to give Andi and Buffy the most beautiful henna tattoos they had ever seen—one on the back of Andi's left hand and the other on the back of Buffy's right hand.

"They're gorgeous," Andi told Tara when she'd finished. "Thank you so much! What do we owe you?"

Andi reached into her backpack to get out the money Bex had given her earlier and plunked down some cash. "Is that enough to cover the tattoos and the lunch check from yesterday?"

Tara's smile instantly faded. She stared at the turquoise ring, twisting it on her finger, looking forlorn.

"Or, hey," Andi added, "maybe you can keep the ring a bit longer, especially if you think it's making that much of a difference in your work."

"Yesss?"

"Yes!" Andi smiled. "We can figure out a time to meet up and get it back from you—maybe on our way down the mountain tomorrow, if you'll be at the diner?"

"Oh, yesss! I will, I will! Thank you, thank you!" Tara

said, handing Andi's money back to her. "No charge for the tattoosss."

"Seriously?" Andi asked.

"Ssseriously!" Tara smiled.

After they emerged from the tent, Buffy immediately turned to Andi and said, "Okay, that woman was *crazy*!"

Andi smiled and looked down at her hand. "You mean crazy talented, right?"

"How did you know I was gonna say that?" Buffy asked, striking an indignant hand-on-hip pose.

"Because you're my best friend, and because we've been best friends forever—hence the leaves and vines!"

"Oh, right. Thanks." Buffy half smiled.

In spite of what Andi had thought was a pretty significant bonding experience over the henna tattoos, she got the feeling that something was still bothering Buffy. Andi *had* to find a way to make her friend feel better! But how?

"So where to next?" Buffy asked.

Andi knew just the place.

Chapter 26

En route to the Skyscraper Slide, Andi went on and on about how Buffy was going to have the most fun she'd ever had in her entire life. But when they arrived at the line of people waiting to go on the slide, Buffy dropped her head back, her eyes traveling up, up, up to the top, and literally snorted. "No way you went on *that*!"

"I did! I promise! And *you're* going on it, too," Andi countered.

"You know I'll never turn down a challenge, but that? I dunno. . . ." Buffy shook her head, a hesitant look on her face.

But Andi wouldn't take no for an answer. She grabbed Buffy by the hand and pulled her over to join the line, just as she noticed Bex, Ham, and CeCe approaching.

"Hey, kids!" Ham swiveled his hips and moved his fists in a circular motion as he dad-style boogied over to where Andi and Buffy were standing. "What's happening?"

Most kids—and grandkids—probably would have been embarrassed by Ham's moves, but Andi couldn't possibly feel anything but giddy that Ham was there with CeCe, getting an opportunity to re-create some of those unforgettable memories from their youth.

"I'm trying to convince Buffy to go on the Skyscraper Slide with me," Andi replied, giving Ham a quick hug.

Ham turned around and looked up. "Awesome!" he gasped, then extended his arm toward CeCe and Bex. "Come on, girls. . . . We're going up!"

"Oh, no you're not." CeCe shook her head and glanced sideways at Andi. "And neither are you!"

Andi smiled and hugged CeCe hello, then said, "Oh, yes I am—I already went on it like ten times yesterday."

"What?" CeCe spun around and glared at Bex. "This is *precisely* the sort of thing I was *hoping* you would be responsible enough to stop her from doing."

Bex shrugged. "Well, Mom, I decided it might be better

to give her a bit of independence and let her be responsible for her own decisions, and guess what? Ten slides later, it appears that she not only survived—she *thrived*. Have you ever seen this girl looking more confident, self-reliant, self-assured?"

CeCe scowled and turned back to Andi, who did feel like she was glowing with a new sort of confidence when she thought about conquering the slide again. CeCe's face softened. "Hmmm. She does seem okay."

"So! Let's do it!" Ham interjected, grabbing CeCe's hand. "You game?"

"No, I am not—and neither are you," she snapped. "It's one thing for a thirteen-year-old girl to go on a ride like that, but quite another for someone *your* age."

"You mean *our* age?" Ham chuckled.

CeCe tightened her lips and crossed her arms.

"Well, you can stay here, but I'm going," Ham said with a shrug.

Andi grinned, spinning around to look at Buffy. "If Pops can do it, you *have* to do it."

Buffy still seemed unsure—but before she could

make up her mind one way or another, Cyrus and Jonah walked up.

"Hey, hey, hey!" Cyrus grinned and put an arm around Buffy. "Whasssuuup? You guys missed a *killer* show—kind of literally. I mean, nobody died, but Tombstone Playground *definitely* killed it. Knowwhutahmsayin'?"

Buffy smirked. "Um, yeah. I think we do."

"Are you going up?" Jonah asked Buffy and Andi, his eyes sparkling as he looked at the slide.

"Yes! We *are*," Andi said, her eyes challenging Buffy. "Right?"

Buffy shrugged. Why was she being so indifferent? Andi had been pinning her hopes on scary-slide bonding being the thing that finally got Buffy 100 percent over whatever it was that was bothering her, but Buffy seemed determined to punish Andi by *not going*.

Perhaps sensing Andi's disappointment, Bex stepped up. "I'll go up with you guys."

"You will?" Andi's face brightened. "That would be awesome!"

"Cool!" Cyrus grabbed Buffy by the arm, apparently

relieved that nobody was going to try to talk *him* into going down the slide. "Buffy and I will handle the videography over . . . *there*." Cyrus pointed to the waiting area.

"Really?" Buffy suddenly looked mortified.

"Well, somebody's gotta wait at the bottom to catch them if they fall, right?" Cyrus replied.

CeCe smiled and shuttled Buffy and Cyrus over to the waiting area. "Right! Exactly right!"

After making the climb to the platform, Andi turned to Bex, Jonah, and Ham and asked if any of them wanted to go first.

"That's okay—you're the master of the slide now," Jonah said with a smile that made Andi's heart beat with pride.

"Yeah, you go ahead," Ham quickly agreed.

"We'll be right behind you," Bex added.

So Andi hopped onto the slide and held her hands up in the air while screaming the whole way down.

"That was so awesome!" Andi squealed as Cyrus gave her a high five at the bottom.

Buffy kept her phone trained on the slide and barely

acknowledged Andi, apparently taking her role as videographer quite seriously. CeCe's attention was also focused on the slide, but she had a far more worried expression on her face. Jonah went next, giving Andi and Cyrus both fist bumps when he got to the waiting area. Then Bex made the drop.

"Oh my gosh, you were right!" Bex gushed, racing over to Andi. "That was *incredible!*"

"Right? I knew you'd love it!" Andi laughed, turning back to the slide and positioning her phone so she could get a video of Ham taking the plunge.

"Whoo! WAHOOOOO! YEEEEAAAAHHHHH!" Ham was whooping and hollering so loudly as he made his descent, Andi was certain he could be heard all over the Mountain Jam festival grounds. But when he hit the bottom, he made an even louder and far less enthusiastic sound. "AAAAAHHHHHH! OOOOOOWWWWWWW!"

"Ham? Oh, Ham! What did you do?" CeCe screamed, running over to the base of the slide, where Ham was wincing in pain, clutching at his ankle.

"I'm sorry," Ham gasped, staring up at CeCe. "I should have listened to you."

CeCe frowned. "Is it broken?"

"I don't know," Ham groaned. "I don't *think* so."

Moments later, two big guys in yellow EVENT STAFF shirts ran up with a stretcher and rolled Ham onto it. "We've got you, sir," one of the guys said. "We'll have you to the first aid tent soon."

"Thanks," Ham replied.

As the guys carried Ham through the crowd on the stretcher, Andi and the rest of the group followed close behind.

"Here we are, sir," one of the guys said as they lowered the stretcher down and carefully slid Ham off so he was lying on his back in the grass.

"But . . ." Andi's eyes darted around, in search of the first aid tent. She didn't see it anywhere. The guys had simply set Ham down at what appeared to be the end of an extremely long line of people. "Where's the first aid tent?"

One of the stretcher guys looked at her as though she were crazy. "It's up there." He pointed to the front of the line—a spot that must have been at least a quarter mile away.

"Are you kidding me?" Andi scowled.

"Nope."

"You *must* be joking," CeCe said, stepping in. "He's hurt! He may have broken something! He needs to get in there right away!"

"Yeah, you don't think these people all feel the same?" the guy replied, motioning to the line of people who were all obviously in various states of distress.

CeCe quickly realized that she wasn't going to be able to argue her way into skipping ahead. "Fine," she huffed, taking off her small leather backpack and reaching inside as the guys with the stretcher got another emergency alert and ran off. "At least I brought some first aid of my own!"

Ham tried to sit up on his elbows and smiled gratefully as CeCe set the backpack next to him and crouched on the grass to search through it.

"Don't worry, I'll get you fixed up in no time," CeCe

promised, pushing back the dark blond hair matted to Ham's forehead.

After a few minutes of riffling around in her bag, CeCe sat back in frustration. "I can't believe it."

"What's wrong, Mom?" Bex asked, kneeling next to her.

"I had some ibuprofen in here—I was sure of it!" CeCe replied, turning back to the bag to search through it again.

"Oh—I can do better than that!" Bex said, taking off her own backpack and locating the safety-first kit. Moments later, she produced an instant cold pack, which she activated and placed in a thick ankle wrap. "Here, Dad, let me see your ankle."

As CeCe, Andi, and Buffy looked on, Bex proceeded to expertly wrap Ham's ankle. Then she got some ibuprofen from her safety-first kit and handed him a couple of those, along with a bottle of water.

"Thank you, Bex," Ham sighed, already starting to look a bit better.

"Yes." CeCe turned to give Bex a half smile. "Thank you."

"No problem," Bex replied. "I'll just run up to the tent now and see if they can give us some crutches."

CeCe's face brightened and she shook her head. "You sure are full of surprises, Rebecca."

"So I've been told!" Bex gave Andi a quick wink before disappearing into the crowd.

Chapter 27

Back in the Orchid Arena a few hours later, CeCe and Ham were enjoying the opening band. She bobbed her head to the music and held his hand while he kept his foot elevated on one of the white leather massage chairs. It had taken a while to get to the first aid tent, but they eventually made it and were advised by one of the doctors that it was only a sprain; however, that still meant he would need to stay off his ankle and continue to apply ice.

Bex and Andi exchanged amused looks as they watched the older couple.

"CeCe seems like she's actually having fun," Bex observed.

"Apparently, she used to love a good festival," Andi said, shaking her head in disbelief. "Who knew?"

"So how excited are you to see Bowie up on that stage?" Bex asked with a sly grin.

"So excited." Andi couldn't believe it was actually going to happen.

"Me too." Bex smiled. "Should we go join the others?"

Andi nodded, quickly glancing back at CeCe and Ham—who were clearly off in their own giddy, romance-filled world—before she and Bex made their way toward the edge of the stage, where Buffy, Cyrus, Jonah, and Mona had staked out a perfect spot to watch the Renaissance Boys' performance.

Andi smiled at Buffy and grabbed her hand. "Isn't this *amazing*?" Andi asked.

Buffy nodded and forced a smile but then dropped Andi's hand and turned to whisper something to Cyrus. Andi's heart sank. Why was Buffy *still* so upset with her? Tears stung her eyes.

But as soon as the sound of the first guitar riff rang out and all the stage lights started to flicker, Andi felt as though she might cry tears of joy. As she watched Bowie strutting out onto the stage, clapping his hands and waving to the crowd, the goose bumps kicked in and her stomach dropped in the same way it had when she'd gone down the Skyscraper Slide. Her dad looked so energized, strutting around in his black leather pants and vest, grabbing the microphone and shouting "Whaaasuuuup, Mountain Jammers?" before launching into the first song of the set. It was one of the band's hit rock anthems, and Bowie's face broke into a smile as bright as the stage lights when he realized how many fans in the audience were singing the chorus along with him.

After he wrapped up the first song, Bowie paused to take a swig of water and then put his palms together, bowing to the crowd. "I know that a lot of you came to Mountain Jam expecting to see Rafe up here tonight, and I know a lot of you are worried about how he's doing," he said into the microphone. "The good news is that he's gonna be fine—and in the meantime, I'll do my best to do right by him. Thanks for letting me be a part of your festival experience!"

As the crowd whistled and cheered, the band went into the next song—a slower ballad that Andi felt certain was every bit as good as when Rafe sang it. And each time she thought Bowie's performance couldn't possibly get any better, he would glance down and lock eyes with her and a different kind of smile from the one he gave the rest of the crowd would brighten his face. Then, about a dozen songs later, before Andi realized what was happening, Bowie was thanking the crowd, waving goodbye, and walking offstage.

"What?" Andi's face clouded over, and she looked at Bex. "How can they already be finished?"

Bex put her fingers in her mouth and whistled a few times, then turned to Andi and yelled, "Don't worry—they'll be back!"

"They will?" Andi shouted. "How do you know?"

"I just know." Bex smiled and threw her arms in the air. "More! More!"

"Oh!" Andi followed suit, chanting along with the rest of the crowd. "More! More!"

Sure enough, a few minutes later, Bowie was running back onto the stage and the rest of the guys were picking up their instruments as they waved to the crowd.

"Thank you *so* much!" Bowie yelled into the mic. "You really know how to make a guy feel good up here, so we're gonna do one more for you."

As everyone in the crowd jumped up and down, dancing and singing along, Andi gazed up at Bowie. He was singing his heart out, living his dream—and then, as the instrumental part of the song hit, Bowie walked over to the edge of the stage, squatted down, and reached out. Andi's eyes grew wide. Did Bowie want her to get up onstage with him? At first she shook her head . . . but Bowie nodded emphatically and motioned for her to hurry.

"Go on, Andi! Get up there!" Bex said, squeezing her arm.

"Dooo eeet!" Cyrus agreed, giving her shoulder a little push.

She spun around to look at Bex and her friends, all waiting to see what she would do. Andi squeezed her eyes shut and shook her head again but then grabbed hold of Bowie's hand and let him pull her up. Sure, she'd danced in front of people before, but this was different—and kind of terrifying. There were thousands of people out there! She glanced over at Bowie, slapped a hand over her eyes, and then finally went for it. Following along with Bowie's moves and throwing down some of her own personal favorites, she danced harder than she'd ever danced before.

"Whoo!" Bex squealed. "Go, Andi!"

As she continued to dance, Andi looked down at her friends again and noticed that Jonah was staring up at her in complete awe. Andi smiled so hard her cheeks hurt. At last, she had proven to him that she was *anything* but boring. She was the kind of girl who went on crazy road trips on the back of Bex's motorcycle, who went down giant slides, who got up and danced onstage with the Renaissance Boys . . . and she even would have entered the pizza-eating contest if Jonah hadn't started to feel sick! But as cool as it was to know that Jonah was finally seeing her in a new light, the best feeling of all was that *Andi* saw herself differently. More than that, she *felt* different—a bit stronger, a bit wilder, and a lot bolder.

In fact, she wasn't just the kind of girl who would dance onstage with the band, Andi decided; she was the kind of girl who would pull other people up onstage to dance *with* her! But as she looked from Jonah to Cyrus, Bex to Buffy, she was torn over whom to grab. She knew Cyrus would be a hilarious dance partner, and Jonah would be beyond stoked to be up onstage with the band. Of course, Bex seemed like the natural choice to get up there with her and Bowie—a mini family affair. But that's when Andi caught a glimpse of her henna tattoo, illuminated beneath the stage lights, and then looked down at Buffy as a spotlight also shined directly on Buffy's tattoo.

Andi glanced at Bex one last time. She looked so happy! Then she glanced back at Buffy, who still seemed so bummed out. But as soon as Andi reached out and grabbed Buffy's hand, it was as if she had sprinkled magic fairy dust on her, finally turning her back into the best friend Andi knew and loved. Together onstage, they threw down all the crazy moves they'd come up with during all the sleepovers they'd had throughout all the years of their lives. And even after everything they'd been through as friends, being up on that stage together was by far the absolute *most* fun Andi and Buffy had ever had.

Chapter 28

As soon as the set wrapped up, Andi and Buffy and the rest of their group were immediately shuttled over to the side by a huge guy in a black T-shirt with CREW in white letters on the back, who told them to follow the band. Ultimately, after winding past all sorts of equipment and gear and down several dark corridors, they came to a huge tent with a sign that read BAND ACCESS ONLY.

"This is *insane*," Buffy gasped, grabbing Andi's hand as they followed the band.

"Right?" Andi shivered and glanced over at Buffy. "Can you believe we just danced onstage with the Renaissance Boys in front of, like, a million people?"

"I really can't." Buffy pulled Andi aside while the others followed the band into their private backstage tent. Then Buffy puffed out her lower lip and blinked back a tear as her eyes locked with Andi's. "I'm sorry I've been so upset with you."

Andi let out a huge sigh of relief. "And *I'm* sorry I let you down by forgetting about those plans we made, or by lying about forgetting them, or . . . you know. I never, ever meant to disappoint you, and it kills me that I made you so mad."

"Honestly? I'm kind of surprised at how much it bothered me," Buffy admitted. "I've actually been thinking about it a lot, and I realized that it may have been less about you forgetting our plans and more about feeling like we were drifting apart."

Andi frowned. "Drifting apart? *Really?*"

"I know it may sound silly," Buffy admitted. "But I've been pretty busy lately with basketball, so I know I haven't been able to hang out as much. But I couldn't tell if you noticed . . . or cared. And when you said you were going to Mountain Jam with Bex? It didn't just feel like you had forgotten about our plan to go together. It felt like you had forgotten about *me*."

Andi smiled. "Buffy! I could never forget about you!

Our friendship is everything. And I'm really proud of you for being on the basketball team, even if it means you're too busy to hang sometimes. I don't want to make you feel bad about it."

Buffy smiled back at her. "I know I shouldn't have gotten mad when I was really just sad. But sometimes when I'm feeling hurt, it comes out as anger instead. I guess the point is . . . I miss you. A lot."

Andi gave Buffy a hug. "I miss you, too—and I would have missed you more than you could possibly know if I hadn't been able to get you up here this weekend."

"I'm so glad it all worked out," Buffy said.

"Me too." Andi held up her left hand and pressed the back of it against the back of Buffy's right hand. "I mean, which of my other friends would have gotten a matching henna tattoo with me?"

"Obviously not Cyrus!" Buffy smiled.

Andi laughed, and then she and Buffy both did their best Cyrus impressions in unison: "Wouldn't want to get *erased from the Goodman family cemetery plot . . . forevah!*"

"Seriously, though," Andi added, "maybe we should commit to making more time for each other, even when we get crazy busy. Because I don't ever want to forget about you, and I don't ever want you to forget about me, either. You're my best friend. Forever."

"Phew!" Buffy laughed. "Am I glad we cleared that up! So do you think that after we go backstage, we could go back to the Skyscraper Slide . . . just you and me?"

"Oh my gosh, *yes*!" Andi bounced up and down. "I would *love* that!"

"Yay!" Buffy grinned, tilting her head toward the band's private backstage tent. "Then let's *do* this thing!"

After they joined Bex and the others inside, Andi and Buffy saw the guys in the band hanging out at a long banquet table, where they were grabbing bottles of water from a big metal ice bucket and dumping them over each other's heads. Then they all exchanged high fives and fist bumps as Bowie shook some of the water out of his dark curls.

At that point, more people streamed into the tent, including Ham on his crutches, along with CeCe and others who were apparently family members or friends of the other guys in the band. As everyone crowded around, grabbing food and drinks from the banquet table and hugging each other, Andi pulled Bowie aside.

"Dad," she began, and Bowie's face instantly lit up, just as it had when she'd recently called him Dad on his birthday and whenever he had looked at her from the stage—as if the rest of the crowd had fallen away and she was the center of his universe. "Thank you so much for this weekend."

"Are you kidding?" Bowie said softly. "Thank *you*—for talking Bex into taking you, for talking *me* into getting up on that stage."

Andi scrunched up her face. "*I* didn't talk you into that!"

"Um, yeah, you did." Bowie smiled. "You had a whole master plan, and it totally worked, and you know it."

Andi shrugged. "Okay, you might be *kind of* right about that."

"Uh-huh." Bowie gave her a long hug.

"So was it everything you hoped it would be?" Andi asked after they had pulled apart.

"Truth?" Bowie asked.

"Truth." Andi nodded.

"Everything I hoped it would be and more," Bowie assured her. Looking into his light-brown eyes, she once again got the feeling that he was 100 percent focused on her.

Andi smiled and glanced back at Jonah, who was chatting excitedly with one of the roadies. Then she looked over at Bex, who was hugging CeCe while Ham beamed with pride. Finally, she turned and caught a glimpse of Cyrus trying to convince Buffy to *pretend* to dump water on his head with an empty bottle while Buffy just rolled her eyes and laughed.

"Me too," Andi said, turning her attention back to Bowie. "*A lot* more."

Chapter 29

Late Monday morning, after making the trip down the mountain—thankfully, with no flat tires or queasiness, and just a brief stop to get Bex's ring back from Tara at the diner—Andi and Bex arrived at their apartment, happy but exhausted.

"So how did this Mountain Jam compare to the other times you've been?" Andi asked as Bex pulled open the sleeper sofa and they both stretched out. She knew it had been a pretty incredible weekend, but she had nothing else to compare it to—unlike Bex, who'd had about *thirteen years'* worth of other adventures

"Way better!" Bex replied, turning onto her side to face Andi. "In fact, not only was it the best Mountain Jam I've been to, I'd say it was the best music festival, best road trip, best adventure, period!"

Andi smiled while Bex kept going. "I mean, hello? In addition to getting the full VIP treatment, we got to see Bowie perform for thousands of people, I got to see *my kid* dance in front of thousands of people! Plus, going backstage? So awesome! Not to mention all that incredible food . . . getting glitter makeovers . . . those fantastic art installations . . . and our amazing tent!" Bex shifted on the mattress, and the springs creaked. "I sure am gonna miss that bed," she added with a faraway look in her eyes.

Andi laughed. "It really was awesome," she agreed, "and I don't just mean the bed."

"But you know what I think I liked best of all?" Bex asked.

"Hmmm?"

"Getting to experience it with *you* and getting the chance to prove to myself—and to *CeCe*—that I really can be a responsible mom," Bex said. "Even with some sketchy stuff along the way, we're back home safe and sound. I kept you alive the whole weekend!"

Andi was about to laugh when her stomach suddenly made a loud growling noise—even louder than it had when

Jagger had given them a lift in his truck on Saturday.

"Um, was that your *stomach*?" Bex asked, staring down at Andi's belly.

"Yeah." Andi grimaced. "Apparently, keeping me alive requires *a lot* of food."

"Like mother, like daughter," Bex replied with a smile.

"Yeah, but why have I been *so hungry* lately?" Andi wondered. "I can't remember a time when my stomach has been quite so . . . communicative."

"You're probably going through a growth spurt," Bex noted. "In fact, pediatric research has shown that most girls have a major growth spurt between the ages of ten and fourteen."

Andi grinned. "Wow, you sound *just* like CeCe!"

Bex grabbed a pillow and whacked Andi over the head.

"So . . . pizza?" Andi proposed.

Bex cringed. "Ugh. No way."

"*Really?* Why not?"

Bex rolled off of the sleeper sofa and walked over to the yellow trunk that served as an accent table, grabbing her memory box and carefully opening it. "There's something I may have left out when I was talking about all the things that made this Mountain Jam even better than the others. . . ."

"Yeah?" Andi's eyes grew wide. "What is it?"

"I entered the pizza-eating contest again!" Bex revealed, her eyes sparkling.

"WHAT?" Andi felt a mix of emotions—happy for Bex but bummed that she hadn't gotten to go through with it herself, or at least watch Bex compete.

"Uh-huh." Bex smiled mysteriously, reaching into her leather backpack. She grinned as she pulled out a large blue ribbon, which she dangled over the open memory box. "I was going to tell you right after it happened, but you were off somewhere with Jonah and then there were all those bands to see, and before I knew it the weekend had completely flown by, but . . . well . . . you're looking at this year's *first-place winner!*"

"Oh my gosh! That's amazing!" Andi hopped off the bed, barely able to contain herself as she ran over to check out the ribbon, which confirmed—as if there were ever any doubt—that her mother was, hands down, the coolest mom *ever.* And she knew with absolute certainty that neither of them had to worry about being bored—or boring—ever again.